NOWHERE

marysue g. hobika

Dedication

I dedicate this book in loving memory of my mother, Shirley Goodburlet.

Chapter One

Mike

"I can't wait to get out of this stupid car!" I complained for the millionth time. "This ride feels like it's never going to end."

My younger sister, Emma, grumbled her discontent from the backseat—I wasn't the only one who wasn't having a good time.

"We just crossed the state line into New York." My mother gave us a reassuring smile. "It won't be long now, only about two more hours until we reach your grandfather's house. Let's try to enjoy what's left of our trip." Mom slipped in a CD from her favorite musical and began to sing along.

I took her advice and tried to relax. Leaning my head back, I closed my eyes. The top was down on her convertible. The cool air soothed my frayed nerves. After a few moments, I removed the elastic tie from my hair and allowed it to blow freely around my face. Even though I hated every minute of this cross country trek, my mom's bright blue Audi S4 was a fabulous ride. The rush of the wind and hum of the music lulled me to sleep.

My eyes fluttered open when the car slowed. We were no longer speeding down the highway. *Welcome to Railroad*

Mills the sign read. My stomach grew queasy. I feared I might throw up the greasy burger and fries I ate for lunch.

Railroad Mills—or as I like to call it, Nowhere—was established before electricity, and the small town hadn't changed much since its inception. In the center of town, in lieu of a traffic light, was a tall statue of a man. Unless you were from here, you had no idea who had the right of way.

A row of rundown antique shops, a video store, an ice cream stand, a gas station, and a five and dime——*whatever that was*—made up Main Street.

As if this wasn't bad enough, my grandfather, who we called Pop-Pop, didn't live in town. His place was another two miles out, where there was nothing but cornfields.

What am I going to do here? I was a city girl, not a country bumpkin. I liked the sound of traffic and sirens. Here, nothing but silence filled the air. This town was so small that if you blinked while driving through, you might miss it altogether. Dread washed through me.

Emma, who never agreed with me on anything, said exactly what I was thinking. "Mom, are you sure about this? Do you think moving here's really a good idea? Couldn't we just visit for a week or two, and then go back to California?"

"No, we can't go back," replied my mom.

Emma and I exchanged looks of dismay, but before we could argue further our mom continued.

"You'll see, this is the right place for us." She smiled gently, even as her hands gripped the steering wheel. "I know it doesn't look like much, but you'll like it here. Once you've given it a chance."

She was right – this place didn't look like much. However, she was wrong about me ever liking it here. I knew Nowhere would never feel like home.

My mom scanned our new surroundings and took a deep

breath. "And don't forget about Pop-Pop. He needs us." I noticed a hint of sadness in my mother's eyes. "He's been lonely and depressed ever since Meema died."

"That was three years ago, and he's been doing fine without us," I reminded her.

"Well, things are different now."

"That's an understatement," I grumbled. "First, Dad dies, and now you rip us out of our school and away from our friends to bring us here...to the middle of nowhere." As unfairness consumed me, I couldn't help but add, "This fucking sucks!"

She stomped on the brake pedal and turned to me with an angry look. "Mikayla Mooney, we don't talk like that in this family. You better watch your mouth, or I'll pull over and wash it out with antibacterial gel."

Having had that experience once, I wasn't eager to do it again. But I don't give up easily, and I know how to push my mom's buttons. "Fuck was Dad's favorite word," I retorted smartly.

"Just because your dad, who was a grown man, used that kind of language doesn't mean it's okay for you to, young lady."

"I'm going to be eighteen next month. Then I'll be able to make my own decisions. Starting with jumping on the first flight back to civilization."

Mom ignored me.

We passed a house wrapped in insulation; it had been abandoned years ago, before the siding was ever added. It reminded me of the state of my affairs. I had to try one last time to make Mom see things from my point of view.

"I don't understand why I couldn't stay in California and live with Paige and her family and finish high school there. I'm going to miss the best year of my life, withering in this town. I was supposed to be the art editor for the yearbook. *That's* a huge deal. I waited three years for that position! It meant a lot to me. Not that you care."

"Mike, we've been through this a thousand times. And each time, I get a new gray hair," Mom sighed heavily. She quickly checked her reflection in the rearview mirror. "Look at me." She pulled at a few loose tendrils. "I have gray hairs everywhere now. I'm not going to get into this argument with you again. We're moving in with your grandfather, and that's that."

"I hate you," I screamed.

"I'm sure you do," she replied, looking sad.

Even though I pushed her into feeling as miserable as I did, it didn't make me feel any better.

I watched the clock on the dashboard painfully mark the time. As each minute passed, impending doom closed in on me. Suddenly, Pop-Pop's rundown farmhouse came into view, with its crooked old vegetable stand; the hand-painted sign advertised homegrown tomatoes, corn on the cob, and mums. My stomach did another somersault. I silently prayed for her to drive on by, but she turned at the corner and pulled into the gravel driveway, the sporty convertible kicking up dust.

This town was as different from California as any place possibly could be, like we'd just arrived in a foreign country. My old house was three times the size of the one in front of me. Peeling white paint. A missing shutter. Pop-Pop's garden took up most of the side yard; it looked overgrown. The greenhouse was the only thing on the property in decent shape.

I quickly jumped out of the car as if I thought it was going to explode; the reality was, the only thing about to explode was me.

"What's the rush?" Emma took her time, reaching up to stretch.

I almost knocked Pop-Pop down in my haste, as he slowly made his way to greet us. He looked older than I remembered. His skin was weathered, and what remained of his hair had completely gone white. His weary eyes focused on me.

"Hello, Sarah, how was your trip?" Pop Pop asked Mom in his gruff, crackly voice.

"Not too bad. I'm happy it's behind us. The last few miles were the longest," she said, probably glaring at me as I stomped up the steps and into the house.

There were only three bedrooms, which meant Emma and I had to share the small postage-stamp sized room we always stayed in when we visited. There was just enough space for the twin beds with the matching quilts that Meema had made for us, and one dresser. Where was Emma going to put all of her clothes when the moving truck brought them next week? The thought made me laugh. We were used to having our own spacious bedrooms; it would be a miracle if one of us didn't kill the other by the end of the week.

I looked around the familiar bedroom; it was hot and stuffy. It smelled stale and musty. Probably no one had so much as cracked the window since our last visit. I opened it wide and took a deep breath. It wasn't any more comfortable in this old house than it had been in the car. I blinked back tears. *Nothing's right anymore.*

When I went out onto the dilapidated porch, Pop-Pop was giving my mom and Emma a tour of the greenhouse. In no mood to join them, I looked around at my new surroundings. Corn in every direction. Unfortunately, I hated corn. It was tasteless and messy. I hated how it got stuck between my teeth.

Interestingly enough, smack dab in the middle of the cornfield across the road was a crumbling cemetery, marked off by a twisted, black metal fence. I'd always thought it seemed out of place. Now, I knew how it felt.

I was startled from my reverie by tires crunching on the driveway and fresh dust tickling my nose. Aunt Carol and my cousins, Tyler and Austin, got out of a large, green SUV. They lived just a mile down the road. Another reason why moving here was a good idea, according to my mom. She said it was important to have her sister and our cousins close by during this difficult time.

"Wow. Looks like the town welcoming committee's arrived," I said, my voice full of sarcasm.

Aunt Carol ignored my attitude, and gave me a rib-crushing hug. I could barely breathe as she squeezed me tighter. Her baby powder scent filled my nose and made me sneeze.

She finally released me and took a couple of steps back. "You look more like your mother every time I see you. Why, one would think the two of you were twins, with your matching brown eyes and hair. Of course, your hair is much curlier than hers." She tugged on a curl; it magically sprang back into place. I wasn't a toddler anymore; I hated it when people pulled my hair.

Thankfully, Mom ran out of the greenhouse. "Hi Carol!"

Everyone hugged and exclaimed their joy at seeing each other—everyone except me. I stood apart from the group, with my arms crossed over my chest, wishing I were anywhere but here.

My cousin Tyler approached me. "Holy shit. I can't even imagine how pissed off you must be about all this." He waved his hand to indicate my new home.

"Yeah," I answered sardonically, shifting my weight from one foot to the other.

I went into cultural shock as we all sat down on the front porch. Left with no other choice, I grudgingly sat on the porch swing next to Tyler. He'd grown several inches since I saw him last at Meema's funeral. He wasn't the scrawny, lanky boy I remembered. He'd definitely filled out; he was at least six feet tall, and probably weighed close to two hundred pounds. I instinctively knew he was just as immature as he'd always been. Emma folded her lean dancer's legs under her, sitting on the creaky wicker settee between Aunt Carol—who talked non-stop—and my quieter cousin, Austin. My mom and Pop-Pop sat in matching white rocking chairs.

"First thing Monday morning you should take the girls down to the high school and register them," said Aunt Carol. "I know school doesn't start for another six weeks or so, but it's never too early to get things done. The early bird gets the worm, that's my motto." I rolled my eyes at my bossy relative.

I'd fallen into an episode of the *Twilight Zone*. The only thing missing was the eerie music and host Rod Serling. I glanced around at everyone else, but they all seemed absorbed in listening to my aunt.

"I already told the office that Mike's a senior and Emma's a junior, but you'll need to go down to the school to make it official. Tyler's going to be a senior, too. And my baby Austin will be a sophomore." She reached around Emma to pat Austin on the knee. She actually got teary-eyed. *Unbelievable.*

"I was already planning to go down to the school on Monday," said Mom. "I want to register the girls and start setting up my classroom. I have so much to prepare. I can't believe it's almost August." She shook her head.

"What I can't believe is that you're actually going to be teaching again after all this time," Pop-Pop muttered. "Hell, after all the money I spent on your education, it's about time I saw a return on some of the investment I made in you. You know it was a lot of money for us, Sarah. We worked hard to put you and your sister through college. How much have you ever really worked? What's the ratio? Six years of college and only three years of work."

"That's not entirely correct," Mom argued. "As you know, I've been substituting off and on for the past eleven years. I'm excited about having a classroom of my own again."

"Well, ready or not, September's right around the corner. I sure hope you're up to it, that's all." Pop-Pop frowned at Tyler and Austin; they shifted uncomfortably. Tyler stopped the swing from rocking with his foot. "Kids today have no respect. They're downright lazy, if you ask me." Emma looked completely bored with this conversation. I doubted she was even listening; she was too busy admiring her latest coat of fingernail polish.

"My boys aren't lazy," Aunt Carol quickly responded, placing emphasis on the word *my*. "Why, they've had football practice all week. And everyone knows the first week's always the hardest. They have two practices a day from now until school starts. What do you call the practices again, Tyler?"

"Two-a-days, Mom. They're called two-a-days. Get it? Two practices in one day."

"That's right, how could I forget?" Aunt Carol slapped herself on the forehead. "Well, anyway, my boys are working hard. The coach is trying to weed out all the players that aren't tough enough. You must remember what it's like. You played football, Dad. Tyler's following in your footsteps. He'll be the next great quarterback of the family." And our Austin is the only sophomore to make the team."

"We'll see," Pop-Pop said noncommittally.

"What about you girls?" Aunt Carol asked. "What sports do you play?"

"Isn't it obvious? I'm a dancer." Emma untucked her long legs, stretched them out in front of her, and pointed her toes in an exaggerated arch.

"Hey, you should try out for the cheerleading squad," Tyler said. "My girlfriend's the captain. I can put in a good word for you, if you want."

"Really?" Emma's eyes brightened.

"Sure."

"I was on the dance team at my old school." Emma's enthusiasm dwindled, as if she suddenly realized where we were. "But I'm guessing a school as small as Railroad Mills High doesn't participate in competitions."

Tyler nodded with a sympathetic frown.

"Being on the cheerleading squad would be the next best

thing, I guess," Emma said. "I'd love to try out. I've been taking dance and gymnastics my whole life. If I make the squad, then I'd have instant girlfriends." She beamed.

Tyler pulled out his cell phone. "Okay, I'll call Liz now and find out when tryouts are." He bounded off the porch, the phone already up to his ear.

Having one problem solved, my aunt turned her attention on me. "Well, Mike, what about you? Do you play any sports?"

"No, I'm not the athletic type," I answered proudly. "I prefer charcoal pencils and sketchpads to back flips and pom-poms."

"Oh, honey, that's okay." Carol patted my knee. "If sports aren't your thing, maybe there's a club you could join." She tapped her lips with her index finger. "Let me think...what about yearbook? You're artistic...maybe you could take pictures or help with the layouts and design?"

"I don't think so." The mere mention of yearbook was a painful reminder of the coveted position I was forced to give up. I wasn't ready to throw myself into a project like that here. It would feel like a betrayal, like going out and getting a new dog the minute your old one died. "I don't think I'll have time to join the yearbook staff. Or any other club for that matter. I'm going to be way too busy sketching and painting landscapes, starting with the cornfield across the street."

Tyler climbed the porch steps. "Hey, that reminds me, I want to introduce you to some of my friends tonight." He directed his comment toward both Emma and me. "We're meeting up with a few of the guys from the football team. The cheerleaders will be there too. I've told everybody all about you two, and they all can't wait to meet you." He glanced at Emma. "You'll be able to talk to my girlfriend, Liz, about tryouts. So, what do you say?"

"It's going to be legit," Austin agreed.

"I'll go," Emma quickly agreed. Her answer didn't surprise me because she never turned down an opportunity to be the center of attention.

"Mike?" asked Tyler "You in?"

Ugh. The last thing I wanted to do was hang out with Tyler and his redneck buddies. I needed to call Paige, and tell her all about Nowhere. I made a quick excuse, "I don't think so. I'm too tired from the car ride. I'm going to turn in early tonight." To prove my point, I rolled my head from side to side, trying to alleviate the stiffness in my neck.

Emma laughed. "Nice try, Mike, but you can't be that tired. You slept through the entire car ride today. It's our first Saturday night here," she pled. "You're an even bigger loser than I thought if you don't come out with us."

The swing swayed beneath me. Tyler rumbled, as if he were holding back laughter.

I sent Emma a murderous look. "Believe me, I'm still tired. Riding in a car for three weeks and stopping at every national landmark from California to New York is exhausting. We saw everything from Old Faithful, Mt Rushmore, the Mall of America, to the Henry Ford Museum," I grouched.

"Come on, Mike. Don't be like that. You don't want Emma to have all the fun while you stay here with your mom and Pop-Pop, do you?" Tyler shifted his gaze to where those two leisurely sat.

Finding an opening in the conversation to further her cause, my mom added, "It'll give you a chance to meet some of the kids from school. You might like it here, if you made a friend or two."

"Tyler and Austin have some real nice friends, from respectable families. Your mom's right. You can't just dip your toe in the water, you've got to jump in with both feet. Go and meet the boys' friends. You won't be disappointed, I think it's nice of them to gather all of their friends together just so you can meet them." My Aunt Carol smiled warmly at her sons.

I wasn't looking to make friends here. My plan was just to get through this year and then move on. Also I was skeptical about how great Tyler's friends really were despite what my aunt thought. I remembered seeing a few of them from a distance at Meema's funeral, and I hadn't been impressed. At the time they were wrestling and shouting in the parking lot of the funeral home, oblivious to where they were, until my dad gave them a verbal lashing. I quickly looked around at our small circle before deciding what to do. Curiously Pop-Pop was the only one who didn't try to convince me to go out with my cousins. In the end, I was too tired to argue any further but I still had a hard time forming the next words out that make out of my mouth and hoped I wouldn't later regret them. "I'll go, as long as we're not going to be out too late. I really am beat after three weeks in the car."

"Excellent." Tyler exchanged looks with Austin, making me further question what I had just agreed to. "Oh, I almost forgot to tell you, don't wear anything too fancy." He glanced at what Emma and I were wearing. "This isn't California. What you both have on is perfect."

I was wearing cut-off denim shorts and my favorite purple Hard Rock Cafe T-shirt that my dad bought for me on a trip to Hong Kong. I smiled. "Perfect. I wasn't planning on changing." I had no intention of trying to impress anyone anyway.

Emma, on the other hand, pouted. She loved to show off by wearing trendy and expensive clothes. She asked with disbelief, "Really, Tyler, this is what people wear when they hang out?" She pointed to her sweat shorts and T-shirt from the dance camp she'd attended last summer. We had been riding in the car all day, so she had on her most comfortable clothes.

Tyler nodded. "Yup, it's perfect."

Aunt Carol stood to leave. "Well, I sure am glad you made it here safely."

"Thanks," Mom replied.

"Why don't you all come over for dinner tonight? We're going to barbecue, and then the kids can take off after we eat."

"That's nice of you, Carol, but are you sure? You and Matthew have done enough for us already. We don't want to impose on your dinner plans too."

"Are you kidding? Of course, I'm sure." She pointed into the house. "What exactly do you think you'll find in there? Except for the refrigerator, I don't think the kitchen gets much use."

"Hey now, I pour myself cereal and open a can of sardines from time to time," Pop-Pop confessed.

"It's settled then. Come over at six o'clock. In the meantime, get unpacked and rest up a bit."

"Okay, thanks." Mom and Aunt Carol give each other another hug.

Chapter Two

Dooner

My stomach growled as I pulled into the driveway after lifting weights. I'd gone straight to the gym to work on my legs after football practice. I was in the best shape of my life right now. I couldn't wait for our opening game against the Spartans. I'd been working toward my senior year of football since playing Pop Warner. This season meant everything to me because the scouts would be watching to see if I was good enough for college ball. I was going to prove to them that I was. My whole future was riding on this season. It was my ticket out of town.

As soon as I opened the back door, the scent of homemade cookies assailed me. My mom must have been in a good mood today, because she only baked when she was happy. Sure enough, a hot tray sat on the counter, while she stood up to her elbows in cookie dough. I didn't ask her what's up because I didn't want to jinx it. Around my house, good moods tended to come and go quicker than you could say, "Touchdown!"

I grabbed a cookie and stuffed it in my mouth. "Hey, Mom."

"Hi, Jimmy, how was football practice? You're home later

than I expected."

"Practice was good. Since we only had one practice today, I went to the gym to lift." I grabbed the milk out of the refrigerator and drank straight from the carton.

"James," Mom scolded before handing me a cup. "Use a glass."

I filled it to the top, draining the gallon. I smirked as I held up the empty milk container. "Looks like I didn't need a glass after all."

She smiled and shook her head, laughing. When she was in high spirits, I could see a glimpse of the girl she must've been before marrying my dad. She'd been crowned homecoming queen when she was a senior in high school. I got melancholy when I thought about how different her life could have been.

She noticed me looking at her oddly and a worried look came over her. "I hope you aren't overdoing it. Today was your first day all week with only one practice and you go to the gym afterwards? Haven't you worked out enough for one week? Your body needs rest, too."

"Leave the boy alone, Martha." My dad entered the kitchen, wearing jeans and a dirty white T-shirt. He looked like he was still on a bender from last night. "He needs to work hard if he wants to play pro ball. Hell, he's the best football player this town's ever had." He opened the refrigerator and grabbed a beer, twisted off the top, and drained half the bottle in a single swig. "He's even better than I was back in the day. And look at the size of him. He's already four inches taller than me, and he's not done growing yet."

"He could still get hurt."

"Bullshit! He's the toughest tight end I've ever seen. Not only can he catch the ball and run like hell, he can throw a mean block too."

Even though I hated how my parents talked as if I wasn't in the room, I didn't attempt to join in. I had learned it was better to remain quiet. Suddenly my dad belched loudly, signaling the conversation was over. Grabbing another beer, he walked out.

That was my cue to leave too. I grabbed another cookie on my way. "Mom, these cookies taste great." I took a large bite and swallowed. "I'm going to shower and then head out. I gotta get gas for my truck. Do you need anything?"

"No. Go have fun with your friends."

"Okay." My response lacked enthusiasm. She, of all people, knew I didn't have any real friends. I'd never had any of the guys from the team over to watch football, or simply hang out and talk about girls. I was more of a loner. I knew all the kids at school looked up to me because I was co-captain of the football team, and an A student. I used to get invited to parties all the time, but I rarely made an appearance, so eventually they stopped asking me. As soon as anyone tried to get close, I shut down. I never bothered to explain my standoffish behavior. Instead, I let everyone think what they wanted to.

Less than thirty minutes later, I pulled into the only gas station in town to fill up my truck, Old Faithful. She was a red 1990 Chevy Silverado 1500 series, with two doors and a large bed for hauling shit around. For being rear-wheel drive she handled great, even in winter. I threw snow tires on her and added weight in the back to keep her balanced. I'd nicknamed her Old Faithful because she was dependable and never gave me any trouble. If only I could be so lucky to find a girl with those same qualities.

I was filling her up when I heard giggling from a loud group of girls. Looking over my shoulder, I groaned inwardly. It was Liz, the overly flirty bleached-blonde captain of the cheerleading squad, and several of her friends. I tried to ignore them, but Liz never could take a hint.

She bounced her way over to me, shaking her full and curvy hips more than necessary. "Hi, Dooner." Dooner was short for Muldoon, which was my last name, and was what everyone at school called me. Only my family called me by my given name. "I haven't seen you around all summer." Liz ran her red-tipped fingernails down my arm. I held back a shiver. "Where've you been hiding out? I've missed you."

"Been busy." I shrugged my shoulders noncommittally. Regrettably I hooked up with Liz last year after a football game. We'd won in overtime that night, and I was feeling pumped. She was there and had been more than willing to help me celebrate, practically throwing herself at me. I wished I could have a do over for that night, because ever since then she'd been trying to get my attention. The truth was, she wasn't my type and that was never going to change. She was too loud and aggressive.

"Well, if you're not busy now, we could go for a ride together in your truck You know what kind of ride I'm talking about," she added, pressing up against me and grinding her hips. This girl would stop at nothing to get what she wanted.

I had to make her understand once and for all that I wasn't interested. "No, Liz, we can't. Not today. Not tomorrow. Not ever." I stated firmly, pushing her away. "Don't you have a boyfriend? Tyler?" I reminded.

"Damn, Dooner, when'd you get so self-righteous?" She pouted, sticking out her bottom lip.

There was no way any of her little tricks were going to work on me ever again. "Your friends are waiting for you." I motioned to where they stood. I returned my attention to screwing on the gas cap, dismissing her. She stomped away. Waiting until she left, I finally let out my breath. Liz could cause trouble that I didn't need.

I paid for the gas and walked back to my truck just as Ray, a guy from the team, pulled in. Ray was a likeable dude, albeit a little slow to catch on to things.

"Hey Ray."

"Hi Dooner. Hard practice today, huh?" We shook hands.

"Sure was, but you made it look easy." You're a great defensive lineman. No one's getting through you to score on us this season." I smiled and gave him a friendly punch on the shoulder. "You'll stop them in their tracks."

"Thanks, man. That means a lot coming from you." His eyes brightened. "You're the real superstar, though. We're lucky to have you on our side. I didn't see you miss a single catch today." Ray spoke with a note of admiration. "I know they weren't all good throws. I don't know how you always know exactly where the ball's going to be."

I get uncomfortable when people give me compliments. I know I'm good and I want to be the best I can, but I get self-conscious, worrying I might let someone down when they put me up on a pedestal.

I switched the focus from me to the team. "I have a good feeling about this year." I smiled, hoping for another undefeated season. We have a running tally of forty-nine straight wins, zero losses. "It would be great to hang another banner in the school gym to mark State Championship again this year. We have both an unstoppable defense and a great offensive."

"You're absolutely right." Ray lifted his hand in the air and gave me a high-five. "We're going to blow the competition out of the water!"

I noticed Ray wasn't wearing his usual gym shorts and tank. Instead, he had on khaki shorts and a collared golf shirt. I wondered who he had a date with. "You look good, man." I punched him on the arm again. "Who's the lucky girl?"

"I wish," Ray responded. "I'm meeting Tyler and some of the guys to celebrate surviving the first week of two-a-days." His speech slowed with every word, as if he realized maybe he wasn't supposed to mention it to me.

"So you guys are going out tonight, huh?"

"Um...yeah...well, I guess I thought Tyler already told you." He looked down at the ground and shuffled his feet.

"We...a bunch of the guys from the team...and some of the cheerleaders too, I think... are going out to Lacey Road to party. Tyler's cousins from California finally arrived and he wants to introduce them to everyone."

Tyler and I were co-captains of the football team, but off the field we didn't mix much. Ray already looked uncomfortable. I didn't want to make him feel worse, so I didn't reveal that I hadn't been invited. "Yeah, I think I heard Tyler mention it. He's talked non-stop all week about his cousins moving here."

"Yeah, he has." Ray seemed relieved. "Maybe I'll catch you later then."

"Later," I returned as I climbed into Old Faithful.

Chapter Three

Mike

We'd finished eating barbecue and all the accompanying side dishes at my aunt's house, and now it was time to clean up. I grimaced as I carried in the leftover ears of corn and placed them on the counter.

"Mike, Emma, will you be dears and get towels out of the second drawer over there and dry the dishes please?" Aunt Carol directed. She was busy, transferring the leftovers into plastic containers, while Mom washed the dishes at the big farm sink.

"Sure," Emma and I said in unison. I tossed my sister a towel, and after what seemed like an eternity, the dishes were all dried. I wondered why my aunt never owned a dishwasher. I was about to suggest she get one, when Tyler and Austin entered the kitchen.

"Perfect timing, huh, bro?" Tyler chuckled, looking around the now clean kitchen. "Hey Mike, Emma, are you ready? It's time to go. I told everyone we'd meet them at nine." Tyler looked at the clock on the wall. He grabbed his keys off the hook by the back door and tossed them from one hand to the other. "I don't want to keep everyone waiting."

I hated when guys thought just because they were guys they didn't have to help around the house. My dad always helped out in the kitchen. Every weekend he made us a big breakfast: eggs over easy, with just the right amount of runny egg yolk, and maple flavored sausage, browned to perfection. Just thinking about it made me hungry again. I wished he was here to whip me up some right now.

Sad and frustrated, I took it out on the nearest target— Tyler. "We'd have been done sooner if you'd helped."

"It's okay," he said. "It won't take long to get there. We're meeting everyone just around the corner."

"I'm ready," Emma responded cheerfully.

I was in a bad mood and we hadn't even left the house yet. I tried to think of an excuse not to go, but I couldn't come up with any. "I guess I'm as ready as I'll ever be." I ran my hands over my unruly hair. It didn't matter how I looked, because I wasn't interested in impressing anybody. "Let's go get this over with." My lack of enthusiasm reflected in my tone.

"Okay Mom, we'll see you later," Tyler said.

"Have a good time, honey. And please be careful. You know I wouldn't want anything to happen to my boys."

"Don't worry, we'll be careful. I'll make sure to take good care of Mike and Emma, too."

Emma gave our mother a hug. "Bye Mom."

Ugh. Did she always have to be the perfect daughter? I swore she did this shit just to make me look bad. I simply waved goodbye and followed Tyler out the door.

"Shot gun, double barrel, no blitz," Austin yelled, racing toward the passenger side door of the truck.

What the hell did that mean? Where I came from, we simply said, "shotgun." Again, I was reminded of how different this place was. They spoke a completely different language.

As soon as we settled into Tyler's four-door extended-cab pickup truck, I asked, "Exactly where are we going?" I racked my brain, but sadly, I couldn't imagine what there was to do at nine o'clock on a Saturday night in Nowhere. There were no coffee shops or restaurants open this late, and there was no movie theater or arcade. I wondered if we were going to be spectators at a tractor pull? I didn't even know what that was, but it seemed a likely possibility.

Tyler and Austin exchanged looks again.

"Yeah, where are we going?" Emma repeated when the boys didn't readily respond to my inquiry.

"We're meeting a few of the guys from the team. You'll like them. My girlfriend Liz and some of the other cheerleaders are tagging along too. We're celebrating the fact that we all survived the first week of two-a-days."

"That doesn't answer the question. Where are we going?" I shouted, not bothering to hide I was getting pissed off. I had a premonition we were being led to the slaughter.

"You'll see. We're almost there."

Uh-huh. I saw nothing but darkness and trees. We were even further out in the country than where Pop-Pop lived. Just when I thought it couldn't get any worse, Tyler turned at the next side road and suddenly the ride got a whole lot bumpier. What the fuck, a dirt road? This couldn't be good. A posted sign read, "Road closed from Nov to Mar." Too bad it was only the end of July. Though these guys would've probably ignored the sign anyway. I was beginning to think my cousins didn't have a brain between them.

"This is where we're going?" My voice filled with disbelief. "Is this another one of your sick jokes? Like when we were kids playing hide and go seek, and you pretended to be nice and showed me a great hiding place, except it was right next to a skunk's home. I didn't know that, of course, and got sprayed."

"No, this isn't like that." Tyler laughed. "But that was funny." He was enjoying himself a little too much. "I promise—no tricks tonight." He made a big show of crossing his heart. "As a matter of fact, we're here." He did a U-turn and parked his truck on the side of the road, leaving the

21

headlights on and turning up the radio.

The song playing sounded like a cat getting run over. I didn't understand how anyone could enjoy the sound of twangy country music. "We're here?" I stuttered. "We're out in the boonies, Tyler. Be serious."

"I am." He jumped out. Emma and I exchanged looks before cautiously following Tyler's lead.

"This is where you go for fun on a Saturday night?" Emma asked. "What's there to do out here? Get eaten alive by mosquitoes?" She swatted her leg.

At least I wasn't the only one who thought this was absurd.

Before Tyler could defend himself, another car approached.

"The boys are here," he shouted, a note of excitement reflected in his voice.

"Hopefully, they remembered the beer this time. This is supposed to be a B.Y.O.B. party," Austin noted with sarcasm.

"A what?" I asked.

"Bring Your Own Beer, duh. Last time they didn't bring any, the leeches. Tonight I could only muster a twelve pack, and that won't be nearly enough."

"Wait." I held up my hand. "We're miles from civilization just to stand around and drink beer?"

"Exactly," Austin responded, shrugging his shoulders.

"Don't forget we're also here so you can meet some friends," added Tyler.

"I can hardly wait," I mumbled with sarcasm.

"Hey guys," Tyler called to the three unusually large guys who piled out of a black pickup truck. Tyler shook hands with two of the guys and slapped the other one on the back.

I waited for a secret handshake, but thankfully there wasn't one. "I want to introduce you to my cousins who just moved here. They're going to be starting school with us in September." He led them over to where Emma and I leaned against his truck.

"Hi, I'm Emma." Emma looked at me, standing next to her, and added, "This is my big sister, Mike. Her real name's Mikayla, but everyone calls her Mike."

I didn't need Emma to speak for me, but since I didn't want to be here in the first place, I let it slide.

Tyler introduced us to a guy who instantly reminded me of him. If I didn't know better, I'd think they were brothers. They had the same color hair and similar haircuts, but different eyes. Tyler's eyes were big and brown like mine, while his friend had small hazel eyes. He must be Tyler's best friend. It was weird how sometimes best friends tended to look alike. People were always asking if Paige and I were sisters, and seemed surprised when we told them no.

Sure enough, Tyler introduced him. "This is my main man, Casey. He and I go way back."

"We've been friends since the first day of kindergarten," Casey agreed. "Tyler was so dumb back then he couldn't even read his own name. He took my crayon box instead of his own. I set him straight and we've been watching each other's backs ever since." Casey smiled, which caused his small eyes to close. The rest of the guys joined in the laughter.

I bet this whole town was full of friendships that went way back. Their camaraderie made me miss Paige more than ever.

Tyler continued to introduce us to the rest of his cohorts. "This is Tank." He pointed to the biggest guy. "I wasn't sacked one time last year thanks to him."

"I admit, I don't know much about football, but even I can see why you go by Tank." I raised my eyebrows as I took in the sheer size of him. He was easily the biggest and the thickest guy I'd ever met. I couldn't help but wonder how many grades he'd failed.

"And this here's Ray." Tyler mentioned what position he played too, but I'd stopped paying attention. Ray was the cutest of the three, with shaggy blond hair and clear blue eyes.

Compared to the other guys, he actually looked like he put some thought into what he wore. Unfortunately, he'd doused himself with way too much cologne. I could smell him from three feet away.

"Hi," I said simply, without adding anything more. I wasn't into small talk, especially when it centered around football.

Austin opened the tailgate of the truck and lifted down the cooler. Casey noisily added two six packs and a handful of Smirnoffs that he'd brought.

"We have a whole case now. Hope it's enough," commented Austin.

"Wow, Aunt Carol must really be slipping," I said, peering into the cooler. "What did she honestly think we were going to do tonight, go on a late night picnic?"

Tyler laughed and threw a beer to each of his friends. He held one out to me in a questioning gesture.

"No thanks." I couldn't stand the smell of beer, let alone the taste. The mere thought of drinking one made me nauseous. How anyone could drink the nasty stuff was beyond me.

"What about you Emma, you want a cold brew?"

"Sure."

Say what? Since when did Emma drink beer? She was a dancer who worshipped her perfectly sculpted body. She wouldn't even drink juice, because she said it was too fattening, let alone beer. I shook my head in disbelief.

"You should have one, Mike." Emma tried to coax me into taking a beer.

"No thanks. I'm all set."

"You're such a buzz kill. You know, a beer might help you relax and loosen up a little." She frowned. "You're just afraid to have fun. Sometimes I can't believe we're actually related."

"I know the feeling." I cringed as she took another sip of the foul-smelling brew. I hoped Emma knew what she was doing. If beer smelled that bad going down, I could only imagine the stink of it coming back up. My stomach did a back flip just thinking about it.

Tyler interrupted our argument, shouting in order to be heard over the hillbilly music. "Liz and her friends are here." I watched as two fake blondes and a brunette got out of a Jeep Liberty that just joined the party.

The girl wearing the tiniest tank top and the shortest shorts marched directly over to Tyler, wrapped her arms around his neck, and kissed him hard on the mouth. I even saw a flash of tongue.

I hated public displays of affection. It only proved how shallow a person was. As soon as the make-out session was over, Tyler introduced his girlfriend, Liz, and the rest of her friends to us. Emma joined their little circle to talk about cheerleading tryouts, which left me standing alone in the middle of the dirt road wishing I hadn't come. I should have stayed home and called Paige.

Casey saw me standing by myself and came over to talk to me. "Hey, I'm Casey."

"Yeah, I remember Tyler saying that."

"You're going to be a senior, right?"

"Right."

"Me too. We should hang out together sometime." His gaze went from my face, slowly down to my feet, and then back up.

I didn't like guys checking me out like I was a piece of meat. A shiver shot down my spine.

"I don't think so," I responded harshly. Then I caught Tyler's eye, and he winked at me. I decided to let him down easy, since this was Tyler's best friend. "It's just that I'll be busy unpacking and getting settled in. I promised my mom I'd help her set up her classroom. She's going to be the new freshman English teacher."

"Well, I can help you find your way around school if you

want."

"I'm sure I'll be able to find my classes." Wow, this guy just didn't get it. "I'll tour the school while I'm helping my mom."

"Independent. I like that in a girl," he said, moving closer. His breath smelled like cheap beer and bad bologna. I thought I might be sick. I took a giant step back, but Casey didn't seem to notice and kept right on talking. "You like football, right?" Not giving me a chance to answer, he continued, "I'm a starter. We have two practices a day right now."

"So I've heard." I wondered if he detected my intentional note of sarcasm.

"It's exhausting, but it'll be worth it when we have another undefeated season. Coach is riding us hard so we'll be ready for our opening game against our biggest rival, the Spartans." He barely took a breath, obviously enthused about his football. "I can't wait to see the look on their faces when we crush them." Casey crushed the empty beer can in his hand to emphasize his point. "You'll have to come to the game. Everyone in town comes to watch us win. I play a defense position called free safety. It's my job to read the other team's QB and stop the team from scoring a touchdown. Let's just say, it's usually a total blow out."

Obviously, he'd taken one too many hits to the head. How was it possible for one guy to talk so much and say so little? Did he really think girls were into listening to someone go on and on about themselves? This guy was a real piece of work.

"I don't follow football." I couldn't resist the dig. I had to swallow laughter when he looked at me like I was from Mars.

He quickly shook my remark off and asked, "Would you like to wear my away game jersey to school on the day of our opening game?"

"Excuse me?" I stuttered. What was he talking about? Did he just ask me if I wanted to wear his smelly jersey?

"Well, on game days we all wear our home jerseys to

school to show spirit and get everyone pumped. We each ask a girl to wear our away jersey that same day," he explained slowly, as if I was some kind of an idiot.

There was no way in hell I'd ever wear Casey's—or any other jock's—filthy, sweaty jersey. If this was common practice in Nowhere, then the whole town must be mental. Not to mention the fact that I couldn't care less about school spirit; I didn't even want to be a student at Railroad Mills High. I needed to put a stop to this madness. He hadn't taken the hint when I was trying to be nice. So, I gave him a malevolent look and hissed, "Casey, I'm not interested in wearing your dirty jersey. I'm happy wearing my own clean and boring T-shirts." I gestured toward what I was wearing.

Casey took it as an invitation to check me out again before he said, "Oh, okay, Mike. Just let me know when you change your mind." He walked over to the cooler and grabbed another beer.

I stared at him, thinking he had no reason to be so cocky. I was never going to change my mind about him. He was the kind of guy I stayed as far away from as possible. I let out my breath. Now that he was gone, I could breathe freely again.

Emma cheerfully approached. "The cheerleading tryouts are on Monday." She grinned. "I'm so excited. I hope I make the squad. I mean, why wouldn't I? I've been dancing and tumbling my whole life. These girls are great." Emma seemed so optimistic and bubbly. I wished I've could mustered that much enthusiasm.

Instead I rolled my eyes, but before I could comment, another truck came rambling down the road, its bright headlights aimed at us, momentarily blinding me. A few seconds after the driver cut his lights, I watched as everyone exchanged looks of surprise. Apparently, no one else had been expected at this shindig.

"Ah, shit!" exclaimed Austin angrily. "What's he doing here?" He turned to Tyler. "I didn't know you invited him, too?"

Whoever *he* was, no one seemed happy about his sudden appearance. Immediately, my curiosity was piqued.

"I didn't invite him. Just because we had a good practice today, and he caught all the passes I threw at him, doesn't mean I suddenly want to hang out with him." Tyler shrugged. "I can't imagine how he knew about this."

A hush settled over the small circle of friends. Several seconds ticked by as everyone looked at each other curiously. The only sound was the buzzing of mosquitoes and a low and melancholy voice singing about a broken heart.

All at once, Ray nervously spurted, "Oh, no. Sorry guys. It must have been me. I saw him uptown today at the mini-mart getting gas and I mentioned how we were all gettin' together to meet your cousins." He glanced in our direction. "I didn't know you didn't invite him. I think he's kinda cool," he added sheepishly, looking at his feet while waiting for Tyler's reaction.

"Damn it, Ray! I swear your mama dropped you on your head when you were a baby."

A few of the guys laughed.

Ray's face turned red. "I said I was sorry."

I felt bad for Ray that Tyler was going off on him. As kids, he always had a temper and he'd lash out for the stupidest reasons. Like the time I got his new kite stuck high up in a tree and he screamed at me until I climbed a rickety old ladder to get it down. I guess I thought he would've outgrown that by now.

The mystery man's pickup truck was more rugged and older than the other trucks there. I wasn't prepared for what happened next. The hottest guy I'd ever seen hopped out and confidently strutted over to where we were all standing. My gaze moved upward from his dusty cowboy boots to his strikingly handsome face. I gasped, in pleasant surprise. I hadn't thought it possible for such a combination of good looks and perfect body to exist anywhere, let alone in Nowhere.

He had on faded blue jeans and a long-sleeved button down shirt, the sleeves rolled up to his elbows. His muscles were taut and natural looking, as if they were a result of hard work and not from pumping iron in the gym. He smiled at me when he realized I was unabashedly checking him out. He had the deepest set of dimples I'd ever seen on a guy. I bet they'd be there even when he wasn't smiling. I looked directly into his unusual green eyes and wondered—who was this football-playing cowboy? Where'd he come from? And why didn't anyone want him here?

Chapter Four

Dooner

"What's going on Tyler, Austin...guys...and...girls?" I asked, nodding in turn at each of them until my eyes stopped on an unfamiliar brown-eyed beauty. I knew instantly that she must be Tyler's cousin, because they shared the same color hair and eyes. I could tell right away that she was different. The girl was a breath of fresh air. She looked as out of place here as I felt. For the first time ever, I was glad that I came to a party.

Drop-dead gorgeous, she had a natural beauty, one that didn't need make-up. She was tall, probably close to six feet, with legs that went on and on in the short jean skirt and flip-flops she wore. She stood straight, her head held high, and her hands tucked in her back pockets. Some tall girls slouch in an attempt to blend in, but not this girl. Everything about her screamed confidence. Her long, brown, curly hair was original too, curls going in every direction. I could get lost in that mass of curls. It was impossible to look away. She was checking me out, too, staring at me as if she could see right through to my soul.

"We're hangin' out, drinking beers, and shootin' the shit," Tyler answered. He must've noticed my eyes were still locked on his cousin's because he added, "Oh, yeah...my cousins just moved here from California today. I'm introducing them to everybody."

I didn't waste a second. I walked over to her and extended my hand. "I'm Dooner."

"Dooner?" she questioned. "What the hell kind of name is that?" She shook my hand. Her hand felt soft in my rough one.

Tyler and his sidekicks chuckled.

"Dooner isn't my real name. It's just what everybody calls me."

"Why?"

"My last name is Muldoon, so I go by Dooner for short."

"Do you have a real name?" she asked.

"Of course, doesn't everybody?"

"Well, what is it? It can't be worse than Dooner?"

"My real name is James Scott Muldoon."

"James." She repeated it back slowly, nodding her head. Coming from her lips, it sounded like pure heaven. "I like it. You look more like a James to me than a Dooner." Her smile lit up the dark dirt road.

"Well, now that you know who I am, the question is do *you* have a name?"

"Of course I do. Doesn't everybody?" She turned my words around.

"Well, I'm waiting." I gave her one of my most sincere smiles.

"I'm Mike."

"Mike? What kind of a name is that for someone as beautiful as you? All the Mikes I know have deep voices and hair on their chests."

"Mike is short for Mikayla," she said in a huff.

I could see a fire brewing behind her dark eyes. I liked a challenge. That's been part of the problem with all the girls around here—they were too easy and predictable.

"Well, I don't like the name Mike for a girl. It doesn't suit you. I'm going to call you Mikayla."

"Fine, just don't expect me to answer if you do, James."

I looked down for the first time and realized that I was still holding her hand.

She followed my gaze and quickly let go of my hand. I didn't want to loosen my grip, but I did.

"You're...a friend...of Tyler's?" She stuttered the question, as if she knew there was some friction between her cousin and me.

"We've known each other forever," I answered in an offhanded tone. Now was not the time to tell her that the word *rival* would more accurately describe our relationship.

"Hey Dooner, you want a beer?" Tyler asked, holding out a can. He knew I didn't drink. Ever. He was trying to make me trip up in front of his honey sweet cousin.

"No thanks, man. I'll pass."

"What a surprise," mumbled Casey under his breath.

It was no secret that I didn't drink. Hell, I was sure that was partly why no one invited me to parties anymore. That and the fact I rarely showed up. They couldn't understand why I didn't join them in getting drunk every weekend. I had my reasons for not drinking—I just didn't share them with anyone.

Then I noticed I wasn't the only dry one at this gathering. "You're not drinking, Mikayla?" I looked at her empty hand.

At first she didn't answer. I thought I'd pissed her off because I called her Mikayla and not Mike, but after several seconds she said, "No, I don't drink. It smells repulsive and undoubtedly kills brain cells." She glanced around at the fellow partiers.

I laughed. Wow, this girl was knocking my cowboy boots off. She was full of surprises. All the girls I'd ever hung out with loved getting wasted and acting foolish. I wondered what other unexpected and intriguing qualities she had.

"I agree."

Suddenly another new face came into view. One I hadn't noticed, having been so enthralled by Mikayla. This girl must have overheard my last comment, because she hurried to put her beer down before approaching. "These boys have such bad manners," she said, batting her eyelashes. "They forgot to introduce us. I'm Emma, Tyler and Austin's other cousin." She reached her hand out to shake mine. I didn't feel any heat run through my body like it had when I held Mikayla's hand. I didn't linger over it. I shook her hand, and then let it go.

I could tell Mikayla and Emma were sisters, yet they looked nothing alike. They shared the same mannerisms, and carried themselves in a similar way. They were equally beautiful, but in completely different ways. Emma had shiny, straight, black hair and bright, blue eyes. I could tell she was used to guys being taken in by her. She stepped in front of Mikayla, who simply rolled her eyes and walked away.

"Are you on the football team too?" she asked, squeezing my bicep.

"Tyler and Dooner are the captains." Liz joined in.

"You seem strong." Emma openly ogled me. "What position do you play?"

"I play tight end." I knew Emma wasn't really interested in football, so I didn't elaborate.

Emma kept up a steady conversation, but I could tell she'd had more than her fair share to drink. She was speaking slowly and slurring her words. She mostly talked about California and moving here. I listened politely, but it was her sister I wanted to talk to. I sneaked in a few questions about Mikayla, but I got the feeling they didn't get along.

The entire time, I couldn't keep my eyes off Mikayla. She sat on the tailgate of Tyler's truck, swinging her shapely legs back and forth. I was being hypnotized, and had a difficult time following Emma's conversation. One minute she was talking incessantly, and the next she was flying through the air. Maybe she lost her balance because she was drunk, or perhaps it was a ploy to regain my attention. In either case, I instinctively reached out to catch her before she fell.

"Are you okay?" I asked and noticed Mikayla watching us from her perch. Her dark eyes narrowed; she looked annoyed. Jumping down off of the tailgate, she went to talk to Tyler.

"Yeah, I'm okay." Emma brushed off her white short-sleeve blouse and straightened out her short shorts. "Thanks, Dooner, for saving me. I'd have broken my nose, if it weren't for you."

"No problem." I didn't want to make a big deal of it.

"That was a close call, Emma. I hope you're not that clumsy during try-outs," Liz snapped.

"I won't be," Emma replied with a note of confidence.

Now I definitely thought it was a ploy to get my attention. As soon as the girls started talking about jumps and cheerleading stunts, I approached Mikayla and Tyler. They were having a heated debate.

"Take us home," Mikayla demanded of Tyler.

"Okay. Let's pack it up," Tyler yelled out to the group, appearing to give in.

"Finally." She sighed happily.

"I think you misunderstood me, Mike. We're not going home just yet. We have another stop to make," I heard Tyler inform her.

"What?"

"What's your problem, anyway? It's still early." He pulled his phone out of his pocket and checked the time. "Jesus Christ, Mike, it's not even eleven o'clock. Will you turn into a pumpkin if you're not home by the stroke of midnight?" Mikayla looked furious. I could see a storm brewing behind her brown eyes. I doubted she would back off without putting up a fight.

Tyler continued. "Have you taken a good look at your sister? I can't take you all home just yet. She needs time to sober up."

"I don't give a shit if Mom sees Emma drunk. I'd love nothing more than for her to be humiliated for once. It's about time our mother realizes Emma isn't the perfect daughter," Mike exclaimed. I was right – Mikayla and Emma didn't get along.

"Well, it doesn't matter." Tyler loaded the cooler into the back of his pickup and slammed the tailgate. I stood by, my hands in my front pockets, waiting for an opportunity to join the conversation. "I'm not taking you and Emma home right now."

Mikayla placed her hands on her hips. "What's the plan then? Where's the next stop on this wagon train?"

A sly smile spread across Tyler's face. "Do you remember the dairy farm we passed right before we turned onto the dirt road?"

She shook her head.

"Well, we're going to go cow tipping."

"Cow what?"

"Cow tipping," Tyler repeated, speaking louder this time, as if there was something wrong with her ears. I took a step closer.

Out of nowhere, Casey rushed over to explain. "You have to come. You'll love it. It's the most amazing adrenaline rush." Mikayla stood speechless. "Have you ever seen the movie *Cars*?"

"Yes," she said, slowly.

It was obvious from the look on her face that she didn't understand how the movie related to cow tipping.

"Well, remember when Mater takes Lightening McQueen out to the field to startle the tractors?" Casey didn't give her time to answer. "It's a lot like that, except this ain't no cartoon. These are real cows. You climb over the fence and sneak up on a sleeping cow and tip it over. You have to be real quiet or else the cows wake up and charge you. So far we haven't been lucky, but it sure is fun trying." Casey laughed hysterically.

Mikayla didn't look like she saw any humor in it, and I couldn't figure out what this idiot found so funny either. In between fits, he sputtered, "Last time, Ray got chased by the biggest cow in the field and pissed his pants. I can't help laughing every time I think about it." Casey was almost doubled over.

"Do you have to tell everyone that story?" Ray protested angrily. His face was beet red.

"Please tell me, you aren't serious," Mikayla pled. She glared angrily at Casey, while gently patting Ray's arm. "Cow tipping is the dumbest thing I've ever heard."

"Unfortunately, they are serious," I stated, finally finding an opening in the conversation. "There's no way you can push over a sleeping cow. They startle too easily." I took a step closer. "Not to mention, the average cow weighs over nine hundred pounds."

"Just because your daddy boards a few horses, doesn't make you an expert on cows," Casey snapped.

I snickered. "And watching a 'how-to' video on YouTube does?"

"We didn't think of that, but thanks for the tip, man. We should make our own video and post it. We'll let you know, so you can check it out. We'll get Ray to star in it." Casey slapped Ray on the back. "I bet the video would get a million hits inside a minute."

"Let's go," shouted Tyler, putting an end to the debate. "Mike, Emma, get in."

Everyone scrambled to find their rides. Emma had her hand on the handle of Tyler's truck, but Mikayla remained standing in the middle of the road with her feet firmly planted. Mountains couldn't move her. I stayed in the same spot, mesmerized by her beauty and her tough girl attitude, waiting to see what would happen next.

"Tyler, I'm not going cow tipping. I'm going home." She gazed determinedly down the road.

"Just how in the hell do you think you're going to get there? I already told you, I'm not taking you right now."

"I don't need you to take me home. I'll walk."

"Walk? You can't walk all the way back. It's too dark. You'll get lost." Emma tried to reason with her, pulling her toward Tyler's truck.

Mikayla didn't budge. "No, I won't. And if I do, I'll call Mom to come and pick me up." She pulled her phone out of her pocket and held it up. "Don't worry about me, I'll be fine. All I need is directions. You can do whatever you want. You can go cow tipping with Tyler or walk back with me."

"I can't walk all the way home," Emma whined, but she didn't move to join Tyler and Austin.

"Then don't." Mikayla turned her attention back to Tyler. "I'm not going to change my mind, so you might as well tell me the directions already."

"Suit yourself, Mike," Tyler huffed . "But you're going to be missing a good time."

"I'm sure." She rolled her eyes. I'd noticed she did that a lot.

Impatiently someone laid on the horn.

Tyler quickly gave her directions to their grandfather's farm. She repeated them back correctly on the first try.

I couldn't believe Tyler was going to let her walk back by herself on these unfamiliar roads, at night. The moon and stars were out but it wouldn't be enough to light up the roads. Mikayla wouldn't even be able to see where they were going. She could easily get lost, or worse. Wow, he was an even bigger asshole than I thought.

I spoke up. "You can't be serious?" I said speaking directly at Tyler. "You can't just leave them here to find their own way back to her grandfather's."

He shrugged, "They can come with us, but they don't want to." He looked annoyed.

"I'm not going cow tipping. I can make sure that they get

home." I opened my truck door.

"Cool," Emma said, jumping into my truck and sliding over. I guess that was one yes. However, I knew Mikayla wouldn't be that easy.

Someone else honked their horn and yelled, "What the fuck, Tyler? Hurry up."

"You got this then, Dooner?" Tyler scowled. He didn't look happy about me escorting them home, but he didn't have a lot of options. Emma was already settled in my truck and his friends were anxious to leave.

"Yeah, I got this."

"If anything happens to them, I'm going to come for you," Tyler warned, pointing his finger at me. He left without another word.

Now that the partiers were gone, the night grew quiet. I could hear the sounds of the country under the starlit sky.

I climbed in and started Old Faithful. I pulled around next to Mikayla. I didn't waste my breath asking if she wanted a ride. I knew she'd say no. "I'm going to follow you home just to make sure nothing happens to you."

"I'll be fine," she snapped.

"I know you will." I nodded. "However, I don't think Emma can walk all the way back to your grandfather's. I'll let her ride in the truck while you walk."

Mikayla peered inside my truck. Emma was passed out cold with her head in my lap. Her hair fanned out over my crotch. I knew it looked bad, but that wasn't my fault. Mikayla glared at me.

"How very hospitable of you." Her voice dripped with sarcasm. "You're a real knight in shining armor. First, you save Emma from ruining her perfect face and now you rescue her from walking miles on dark deserted country roads with her stubborn sister."

I smiled, enjoying her fiery attitude. Mikayla had no idea she was the one turning me on.

"Why are you smiling so smugly?"

"It's just that I'd say you sounded jealous," I said to cover up my real feelings. I didn't want to admit that I was attracted to Mikayla, and I knew she wasn't ready to hear it.

"Me?" She gasped. "I'm not jealous. Emma always has a boyfriend, while another one's waiting in the wings. Guys fall under her spell. I mean, look where her head is now!"

"I didn't plan that, she passed out." I glanced down at my lap and groaned. Emma had shifted and her face was buried in my lap making it look like she was performing a sexual act, even though she obviously wasn't. I tried to move her, but it was impossible. She was dead weight. Giving up, I tried explaining, "Look, I'm not into Emma. I'm not saying she's not pretty, but she's not my type."

"Right." She continued to walk briskly without glancing again in my direction. "What is your type then?"

"My type is a girl who doesn't need to show off or always be the center of attention." *In other words, you.* "She'd know how to have fun in ways that didn't involve getting wasted. She'd be clever and witty and could think for herself. She would have long lean legs, curly brown hair, and dark eyes." I grinned. "Do you know where I might find a girl matching that description?"

She mumbled something under her breath I didn't quite catch. I needed to take things slowly. She appeared tough, but I wasn't buying it completely. A con artist could recognize another one when their paths crossed. I left her alone and didn't ask her any more questions. I simply hummed along to my favorite country music station and enjoyed the view. I wanted to give her the space she needed. I wanted her to trust me.

It took about an hour to reach Mr. Jenkins' farm with Mikayla walking the whole way. I couldn't imagine this new life resembled the one she'd just come from. I tried to see the country setting through her eyes, but it was difficult. I'd never been farther than a few hundred miles from my front door. She probably didn't want to be here; maybe that was why she was so feisty.

I pulled my truck over to the side of the road as quietly as possible. The porch light was on, but otherwise the house looked dark.

I wasn't sure what to do with Emma, but for now I carefully lifted her head and placed it back down as I got out of the truck and gently closed the door. Mikayla leaned casually against Old Faithful with her hands in her front pockets, looking like she belonged in my world after all. Maybe I'd get lucky and make her mine. I'd never wanted anyone so much, and I'd just met her.

I approached her slowly; she didn't look angry anymore.

"Thank you," she whispered.

I brushed a loose curl away from her beautiful face and tucked it behind her ear. "You're welcome."

I wanted to pull her close and feel her against my chest, but I reminded myself I had to take things slow. Several seconds ticked by, and then I leaned down and breathed in her scent. I had never in my life smelled anyone so sweet and tempting. I wanted to kiss her. I'd kissed plenty of girls before, but for some reason I was nervous with this one. I was trying to round up my courage and just go for it, when I heard a strange noise.

It took me a second to identify the source. *Oh shit*! Emma! She was about to throw up. I reached the side of the truck in less than a second, and yanked open the door. I carefully pulled her out in one swift motion. But as soon as she was upright, the force of gravity took over and she threw up all over Mikayla, who'd come rushing over to help, covering her in smelly projectile vomit. There was little doubt what Emma had eaten for dinner. I could tell Mikayla was repulsed, because she started to gag, as though she might throw up too. "Plug your nose," I directed.

She took my suggestion and pinched her nose, looking a little less green. "Let's go out by the greenhouse. There's a hose we can use to wash this shit off." She sounded nasal, still squeezing her nostrils.

Between the two of us we helped Emma walk across the yard. On the way, we passed the clothesline and Mikayla reached up and pulled off a clothespin. "Ouch." She grimaced when she clipped it on the end of her nose. Now she had both hands free to help keep Emma upright. She looked so comical with that clothespin on the end of her nose. I wanted to laugh, but I didn't dare.

Mikayla helped Emma wash up because she could barely stand on her own. Mikayla was furious. I didn't blame her. I knew firsthand that it was no fun cleaning up after a drunk. Emma sat on the ground afterwards with her back against an old barrel, quickly falling back to sleep.

I watched as Mikayla used a rag and the hose to clean the vomit off her own shirt. I shook my head, thinking it seemed like a hopeless cause. Quickly giving up, she pulled her shirt over her head. I was not prepared to see her standing there in front of me wearing nothing but a light blue bra with embroidered dark blue flowers and her jean skirt. I sucked in my breath. She was gorgeous.

I turned my back to her, to be a gentleman, and removed my own button-down shirt. I wasn't wearing anything underneath but I thought it was better if I was shirtless than Mikayla. "Here, put this on." I held it out to her while keeping my back turned. My throat was dry and my voice cracked. I was afraid what I might do if I saw her in that sexy bra again. I felt her take the shirt from me; I assumed she put it on. I counted silently to thirty before turning around.

"Thanks for the shirt." She looked shyly at the ground. I noticed she no longer had the clothespin on her nose, but the tip of it was bright red. I had to hold myself back from leaning over and kissing it.

"No problem." I closed the gap between us. "I guess I'm a lot bigger than you." I laughed as I pushed the sleeves up and watched as they fell back down. My fingers accidently brushed her silky skin, and a tingling sensation spread from my fingers throughout my body. I was momentarily speechless. I had never felt anything like that before.

"I...better...get Emma inside." She seemed as affected by my presence as I was by hers. She took a deep breath. "Would you mind helping me get her into the house and up the stairs? I'm not sure I can do it alone."

"I'd be happy to." I grabbed Emma under the arms and tossed her over my shoulder. She whimpered, but didn't wake up. Mikayla held the doors open while I silently carried her sister from the greenhouse into the house and up the stairs to the bedroom. I gently laid her down on the bed Mikayla pointed at. Then I followed Mikayla back downstairs and out onto the porch.

"Thanks, James, for all your help tonight," she whispered. She moved her eyes over my bare torso and blushed. Quickly she added, "Thanks for the shirt. I can run back upstairs and change so you can wear it."

"No need. I'm not going anywhere but straight home."

"I'll wash your shirt and return it to you the first day of school."

"The first day of school?" I frowned.

"If you need it before then, I can drop it off at your house. You'll just have to tell me where you live."

Didn't she realize I wanted to see her before the first week of school? That was five weeks away. Also, there was no way I wanted her stopping by my house.

"I don't need it back before school starts. I have lots of shirts. You can even keep that one if you want." Stroking her arm, I added, "I like it on you."

She blushed and tipped her head down. I swore I thought I saw her take a deep breath through her nose, intentionally smelling my shirt. I hoped it didn't smell bad. When she looked up, she wore a satisfied smile.

"Are you busy tomorrow?" Smirking I added, "I know how much you like to walk and there's a great trail not far from here that I'd like to show you."

She didn't answer. She just stood there with a strange look on her face.

"So, are you busy?" I asked for a second time. I never asked the same question twice, but I was desperate for her to say yes. She took so long to answer I began to worry that she was going to turn me down.

She nervously brushed back her hair. "Really? You want to go on a hike with me? After everything that happened tonight?"

"I wouldn't have asked if I wasn't serious."

"Okay," she whispered. "I'll go."

"It's a date. I don't have practice tomorrow, so as soon as I finish my chores, I'll call you."

She smiled and opened the door, disappearing inside the house.

Chapter Five

Mike

I climbed the creaky stairs for a second time tonight and entered the bedroom I shared with Emma. Thanks to James and his strong back, Emma was asleep. I placed the wastepaper basket next to her on the floor, just in case she got sick again. I never made the same mistake twice. I hoped Emma felt like crap in the morning, and that her head hurt so much she wished she were dead. Then I'd give her hell.

I'd have loved a hot shower, but I knew it would wake everyone up. There's only one in this house. I missed my home in San Francisco, where I didn't have to share a bedroom or a bathroom. If we hadn't moved, I'd be able to jump in the shower without waking the whole house. I angrily peeled off my skirt, leaving it in a heap on the floor, and climbed into bed. James' oversized shirt was comforting, so I kept it on. He was so tall and strong. I hoped by wearing his shirt, my nightmares might remain at bay. I breathed in his scent—soap with an underlying hint of woodsy earth. I closed my eyes and began to sink into my pillow.

Just as I began to fall asleep, my cell phone rang. Groggily, I scrambled for the device before anyone heard it ringing through these paper-thin walls. Who the hell would be calling me in the middle of the night? *Paige.* I never called her. She probably forgot about the three-hour time difference.

"Hi Paige," I said, my voice sounding sleepy to my own ears.

"I didn't wake you, did I?"

"It's one o'clock in the morning."

"Yeah, but you never go to bed before dawn."

"After the night I had, trust me, I was more than ready to call it a day."

"I sense a good story. Do tell."

I pictured Paige in her red bedroom that I helped her paint last summer, lying on her huge bed with her arm under her head and her feet crossed at the ankles.

"Start at the beginning and don't leave anything out," Paige prompted.

Paige and I met in sixth grade, when she moved to our school, and we'd been best friends ever since. She knew me better than anyone. She'd been there for me through everything— my dad dying, all the fights with my mom, and most recently this dreadful relocation. Paige and I had talked on the phone every day since I left San Francisco. I didn't think I would've survived the road trip without our daily phone calls.

I began with our arrival and I finished with Emma getting plastered and puking all over me.

"Wow," Paige said. "Why couldn't Emma save that performance for when I come to visit you for your birthday? I'd pay to see her make a fool of herself. You must be super pissed."

"I'm going to kill her in the morning."

Paige laughed. "From the anger in your voice, I almost feel bad for Emma."

My friend had witnessed countless fights between me and my sister over the years. Emma never came out on top.

"Who am I kiddin'? I don't feel bad for Emma," Paige recanted. "It sounds like she deserves your wrath...But enough about Emma. Tell me more about the rugged cowboy that came to the rescue. Is he cute?"

I pulled the covers over my head and laughed. "When he took his shirt off and handed it to me, my heart started to race. He's so beautiful. He has broad shoulders and a perfect six-pack." I had to stop to catch my breath. Just talking about him sent tendrils of excitement through my body.

"Wow." Paige sighed.

I searched for the right words to describe James. "And he's more than just easy on the eyes. I actually enjoyed talking to him. He's different than other boys. He seems older, more mature."

"You enjoyed talking to him?" Paige sounded surprised. I thought a lot of guys were cute, but as soon as they opened their mouths I lost all interest. Guys could be so egotistical and dumb.

I knew Paige was trying to read between the lines. I couldn't keep anything from her. "We didn't really talk that much. It wasn't so much what he said, it was what he didn't say. He didn't ramble on and on about himself and talk about football like every other guy I met. Mostly I liked how instead of pointing out how ridiculous I was acting, he gave me time to walk off my anger."

"And?" She pressed me for my details.

"I thought he was going to kiss me and then, right on cue, Emma..." I ground my teeth as I said her name. "...started throwing up."

"Oh, the irony!" Paige exclaimed dramatically—she liked to use borrowed vocabulary and phrases from the classic literature she was always reading.

"He asked me if I had plans tomorrow," I whispered.

"Well, what did you say?"

"I agreed to go on a hike with him. He's going to call me in the morning."

"A hike?" Paige sounded confused. She knew I'd never gone on a hike in my life. I walk to and from school, but I'm a city girl. A hike implies nature.

"Yes, he thinks that because I insisted on walking home from the party that I must be into hiking. So, we're going to check out a nearby trail."

All I heard on the other end of the line was shrieking. I pulled the phone away from my ear for several seconds to prevent permanent damage to my eardrums until I was sure Paige had regained control.

"I better let you go so you can rest up for your big hike." She giggled. "And don't forget to call me tomorrow night." Her commanding tone left no room for me to ignore her request. "I want details."

I yawned. "Right. Details. Tomorrow night." I closed my phone. I hoped I would be telling Paige all about how right I was about James being different than other boys. I could almost feel his strong arms holding me close as we shared a first kiss.

Chapter Six

Dooner

My alarm went off at six o'clock this morning and I'd been mucking stalls ever since. I paused for a second to wipe the sweat from my forehead. Even though it was still early, I could tell it was going to be a hot and humid day. I finished laying fresh hay in the last stall. I couldn't wait to be done with my chores. I was so hungry, I could've eaten a six-egg omelet without blinking an eye.

There was plenty of time to eat, shower, and rest before my date with Mikayla. I was so glad I bumped into Ray yesterday afternoon and found out about the get-together to meet Tyler's cousins. That had been the first time I went to a party and actually had fun. I couldn't wait to discover why she was so feisty. Bantering with her almost seemed like foreplay. I grinned at the memory of how hot she looked walking home in the moonlight, her curls bouncing and her sexy ass shaking in that little jean skirt.

I snapped out of my daydream when my dad came toward me. I scowled. It looked like he was carrying an apple in one hand and a cigarette in the other. He threw me the apple from twenty yards away. I caught it and took a crunchy bite. It tasted good, but it didn't even begin to take the edge off of my hunger.

"Good catch, son." He slapped me on the back. I almost choked on the large bite of apple in my mouth. "You got a good eye. I would've been disappointed if you'd missed that. Not to mention your breakfast would have landed in the dirt." He laughed.

"This is my breakfast?" I grumbled angrily, staring at the half-eaten apple. "I'm so hungry I could eat a horse." I swore I heard the horses in the barn whinny. I called out over my shoulder, "Sorry guys, no offense."

"It's all I got." My dad shrugged his shoulders, as if to say it wasn't his problem I had such a large appetite. "Anyway, your mom's too busy this morning to stop and make you something to eat. She has work to do. So do you."

"What do you mean?" I asked, finishing the apple. I threw the core as far as I could.

"Not a bad arm either. You sure got talent, kid." He stamped his cigarette with the toe of his farm boot. "I need your muscle power right now. The tractor has a tire that needs changing."

"Okay," I agreed quietly. I knew there was no way out of it. It would be faster in the long run to help him now and get it over with. It wasn't even 9 a.m. I couldn't call Mikayla yet anyway because she was probably still asleep.

We reached the field where the tractor sat, along with his pickup truck. "What exactly do you need me to do?"

"I need you to help me get the tractor up in the air, so that I can take the tire off. Get the jack." He pointed to the pile of tools. I carried the heavy jack and placed it under the tractor frame near the flat tire. I cranked it according to my dad's instructions. I thought my arm might snap in two; I had to use all of my strength just to get it to budge a few inches. Sweat poured down my back, soaking my shirt. My dad loosened the lug nuts and it took both of us to get the old tire off. Tractor tires weren't light. I sighed with relief when we placed it in the back of the pickup truck.

"Hey, where's the new tire?" I looked around, but I didn't see it. "In the barn?" I was anxious to finish this job.

"Get in," my dad said, closing the tailgate of his truck. I did as I was told. My dad got in too and started the engine.

"Where are we going? I thought the new tire was in the barn?" We weren't headed in that direction.

"No, I never said that." He laughed and lit another cigarette. The smell suffocated me in the small confines of the cab. "The new tire's at the store. You didn't actually think I kept spare tractor tires hanging around, did you?" He chuckled. I never found any humor in my dad's comments.

"We're going to the supply store? Now?" I shouted. I was pissed. How could I have been so stupid to think anything my dad involved me in would be quick and easy? "Can't you go by yourself? The guys at the store will help you unload the old tire and reload the new one. Then I'll help you put the new tire on when you get back," I reasoned.

"Sorry, Jimmy, I'm not turning around." He pulled out onto the main road. Like most places, the farm supply store was at least twenty miles away. We were going to be gone awhile. I let out a frustrated sigh. Today of all days, I didn't have time for this. Luckily, I felt my phone in my back pocket. I'd call Mikayla while my dad was preoccupied looking at tires. Damn it! I didn't even have her number. I'd have to call information to get her grandfather's number.

"All right, stop your fretting," my dad announced, misinterpreting my brooding. "I'll take you to breakfast before we get the new tire. You can order whatever you want, no matter the price." He shook his head. "I never met anyone in my life who thinks about food as much as you do. You're going to eat me out of house and home. That scholarship of yours better include a meal plan," he joked, pulling into a local grease joint.

The smell of dirty oil and fried food hit me as soon as we pushed open the door. The booths were covered in red vinyl and showed signs of wear. Normally I tried to stay away from places like this, but right now I'd eat just about anything. I ordered the special, rightly named the rubbage plate—two hamburgers, mac salad, and home fries. I washed the meal down with a large chocolate milkshake. My dad silently watched me eat, ordering only a cup of coffee for himself.

It was almost noon by the time we pulled into the supply store's parking lot. Half the day was already gone and I still hadn't called Mikayla. I helped my dad unload the flat tire and then I took off in the opposite direction.

I called information and had the operator connect me. The whole time I waited I was hoping that Mikayla would understand why I wasn't going to be able to go on the hike like I'd planned.

On the tenth ring, someone finally answered. "Hello." The person on the other end sounded annoyed.

"Hi, this is Dooner. Is Mikayla there?"

"Oh hi, Dooner. This is Emma,," she responded, her tone changing "Aren't you such a gentleman to call to see how I'm feelin'?"

I rolled my eyes, even though she couldn't see me. "Look, I only have a sec. Can I talk to Mikayla, please?"

"Do you mean Mike? Because she hates it when people call her Mikayla."

"Yes, I mean Mike, Mikayla, whatever. Just please, can I talk to her?" I was starting to get exasperated. My dad would be looking for me soon.

"I'm sorry, Dooner, but she can't come to the phone right now. She's in the shower."

I peered around the corner and saw my dad. I quickly turned down another aisle. Keeping my voice low, I added, "Well, can you take a message for me then?"

"I'd be happy to."

I paused for a second to gather my thoughts. "Please tell Mikayla that I'm sorry, but my dad has me running errands and helping him on the farm. I'm not going to be able to get together like we planned. I'll call back later when I'm done. Maybe I can stop by after dinner, or something." I hated making excuses, but in this case it was the truth.

"Don't worry. I'll make sure she gets the message," promised Emma.

"Thanks," I responded, lacking enthusiasm. I had a bad feeling that Mikayla wouldn't get the message that I called. *She'll probably assume I'm blowing her off.* I sighed, feeling defeated.

I stuffed my phone back in my pocket just as my dad walked toward me. "I'm all set with the tire." He motioned me to follow him. "Come on, I need to grab a few other things while we're here." I felt like my one chance with Mike was gone.

It was four o'clock in the afternoon by the time we were finished putting on the new tire. I couldn't believe how long it had taken. "I'm calling it a day," announced my dad as we put away the tools. He must need a drink, I thought. Hell, if I drank I'd grab one too after the day I had.

I turned on the shower and washed away the sweat and dirt. I felt terrible about screwing things up with Mikayla. I knew I should call her and explain what happened, but I didn't think she'd want to talk to me.

Chapter Seven

Mike

I used my fork to push the meatloaf around my plate. I didn't have much of an appetite. I felt like an idiot for sitting around the house all day, waiting for that cowboy, James, to call. "Can I be excused?"

My mom looked at my uneaten dinner and sighed. "Sure."

I walked out onto the front porch. As the door closed behind me, I thought I heard a kitchen chair scrape across the floor. Seconds later, Emma poked her head out. "Mind if I join you?"

Since when did Emma ask my permission to do anything? "Sure." I shrugged.

Emma lay down on the wicker settee, resting her head on the pillows, and curled up into a ball. She looked like hell. She wasn't wearing any make-up; even though she had olive-toned skin like our father, she looked extremely pale. The corners of my mouth turned up when I realized that she was getting the punishment she deserved.

She took a deep breath. "I want to thank you for taking care of me last night." She continued slowly, talking mostly to herself. "We were partying on that dirt road and Tyler introduced us to some of his friends. I met his girlfriend, Liz, and we talked about cheerleading tryouts." She paused to scratch at a giant mosquito bite on her leg. "We were all having a good time and then out of nowhere you decided you wanted to go home. I climbed into Dooner's truck and that's the last thing I remember. This morning I woke up in my own bed. I assume you had something to do with that?" I couldn't respond because I was too shocked. This was the first time Emma and I had talked all day. She didn't get up until late, and by then I had gone on a walk by myself, realizing that Dooner had stood me up.

Emma added quietly, "Thanks. I don't know what would've happened to me if you hadn't been there. I was pretty drunk."

"That's an understatement."

"I did feel awful when I woke up today." I raised my eyebrows. "Okay, I still feel awful. My stomach's queasy and I've got a killer headache. It's like I was on an upside-down roller coaster ride all night long with my head thrashing against the safety bars while my stomach did loop-de-loops." She closed her eyes.

If Emma was looking for sympathy, she wouldn't find any here. "You deserve to feel like crap."

Emma opened her eyes and pushed up onto her elbow. "What the hell does that mean? I already thanked you for taking care of me."

"Don't you remember what happened after you fell asleep in Jam truck?"

"Who the hell is James?" She sounded confused.

"Dooner, James, whatever you want to call him. Do you remember what happened or not?" I asked for a second time, getting impatient.

"No. Why? Did something happen?" Her voice suddenly jumped an octave. A wicked smile spread across her face. "Did Dooner kiss me? Surely, I'd remember that." She scratched her head. "He is drop-dead gorgeous."

My mouth hung open.

Emma mistook the look on my face. "That's it, isn't it? He kissed me. Don't even try to deny it."

I snickered. "I have news for you. James definitely did not kiss you." I paused briefly before delivering the punch line. "You puked on me."

Emma stood up. "You're such a liar! There's no way I'd throw up in front of Dooner. You just made that up because you're jealous that he likes me and not you. As a matter of fact, he called me today to see how I was feeling." She raised her chin in the air.

My breath caught in my throat. "James called you today?" I whispered.

"Yes. He called while you were in the shower." She raised her chin another notch.

"Why didn't you tell me he called?" I accused.

"Because he called to talk to me."

"Emma, you're lying," I spat at her.

"I'm not lying. He did call, and he talked to me." She narrowed her eyes. "Why would he call you anyway?"

My temperature was rising. I grabbed a fistful of Emma's hair and yanked her off the front porch fast enough to make her head spin.

"Ouch, Mike," Emma yelped. "What the hell do you think you're doing? Let go of me right now or I'll start screaming." She tried shaking me off.

"Shut up!" I yelled.

Emma actually listened and stopped struggling. She must have understood that I wasn't going to stop until I saw this through. I released her. Rubbing her scalp, she followed behind me like a scolded puppy with her head down.

"I'm going to prove to you that you did puke all over me last night." I pushed open the greenhouse door and marched over to the garbage can where I'd thrown my disgusting T-shirt. I pushed her head down into the garbage so that she could get a good whiff.

"What does that smell like to you?"

She stood up and flipped her straight, black hair over her shoulder. "It smells like garbage. That doesn't prove anything." I'd forgotten that Emma could be almost as stubborn as me.

Calmly I put on a pair of gardening gloves that were lying around and reached into the garbage can, pulling out my crusty T-shirt. The puke had dried and it smelled terrible. "Here's the proof you wanted, Emma." I waved the dirty shirt inches from her face. "James was holding you up from behind and I was standing in front of you. When you puked, it landed on me. Ring any bells?"

"I had no idea." She slumped to the ground. Covering her face with her hands, she began to cry.

Suddenly I felt sorry for her. Maybe Emma acted so out of character because she wanted to fit in. She was probably just as scared and unhappy about moving here as I was. I sighed and sat down on the floor facing her. I remained silent for several minutes, unsure of what to say. When she'd calmed, I asked, "Are you okay, Emma?"

Slowly she uncovered her face. Her usually flawless skin was red and blotchy. "No. I can't believe I humiliated myself like that on the first night. Everyone probably thinks I'm a loser." Silent tears continued to run down her face. Emma always worried about what everyone else thought. "I'm sure no one wants me on the cheerleading squad now."

Strangely, I wanted to assuage her fears. "Don't be so dramatic, Emma. James and I are the only ones who know you got sick. I won't tell anyone and I'm sure he won't either."

"What if he already told all the guys on the football team? Before you know it, the whole school will think I'm a lush. My reputation is ruined." She sniffed loudly.

I shook my head. "I doubt it. James won't tell anyone.

He's not the type." *I can't believe I'm saying that when only a half an hour ago I was ready to think the worst of him.* "He wouldn't be that cruel. He was worried about you, just like I was."

Emma's intense blue eyes looked guilty. "Can I tell you something?" she asked and rushed to add, "without you getting mad at me?"

"Yes..." I wondered what Emma was up to now.

"You have to promise not to get mad."

"I won't get mad." My voice rose unintentionally.

"You're getting mad already."

I took a deep breath and let it out slowly. Politely I asked, "What do you want to tell me?"

Emma's face turned even redder. "James did call this morning. Only you were right, he called to talk to you, not me. I lied. He's so good-looking and he has such an amazing body," Emma drooled, "that I wanted him for myself. Sorry. Are you mad?" She ducked her head, covering it with her hands. You're not going to pull my hair again are you?"

"No." I chuckled.

"Phew," she sighed.

"What did he say?" I asked, turning the conversation back to what mattered.

"He asked me to give you a message."

My eyes grew wider in anticipation. I held back from commenting because I didn't want to get my hopes up.

Emma continued. "He said that he was busy working with his dad today and he wouldn't be able to get together until after dinner." My spirits lifted. I hadn't misjudged James after all. He was different from other boys. He wasn't blowing me off; something unexpected had come up.

"Did he say anything else?"

"He said he'd call back later."

Feeling happy for the first time all day I stood up and reached down for Emma's hand. "Come on. Let's go get some ice cream. Mom bought a pint of Ben & Jerry's at the grocery store. It's our favorite—Coffee Heath Bar Crunch."

"Okay." Emma brightened. We looped arms and headed toward the house.

Chapter Eight

Dooner

I was taking a quick water break during the first of two practices on Monday morning. Without pause, Coach shouted the next drill. "Team, huddle up. Let's run wide out drills. I want all the guys who're trying out for wide receiver and tight end to get in formation. Also I need our quarterback, Tyler, out here to throw passes. Let's see who knows how to catch a football." Coach looked at me, the corners of his mouth turning up ever so slightly. I knew he was counting on me this season to catch whatever Tyler threw at me and run for a touchdown.

I wouldn't let him down. Last year I set a new school record for the most touchdowns scored by a single player in one season. This year I planned to break my own record.

I lined up with the other players. It was only a conditioning and technique drill, so we weren't wearing helmets, only light pads and shorts. A couple of drills were run before it was my turn. I stepped up in formation with Casey, Tyler's sidekick, playing free safety. Tyler threw a leading pass. I reached for the ball and caught it easily. Casey plowed into me and I fell to the ground, with him landing on top. I was used to hard hits, but not by my own teammates. I growled. A hit that hard was no accident. It was no secret that we weren't pals, but this was low even for them.

I shoved Casey off of me and stood up. "What the hell was that for?" I shouted angrily.

Casey played dumb. "I was showing Coach I meant business." Coach stood on the sidelines, watching our every move. He didn't look pleased.

"We're only running bump and run drills," I stated, doubting he'd actually forgotten.

Tyler rushed to his buddy's aid. "Hey man, back off."

I turned around quickly and faced him. "What's your problem, Tyler? Why'd you throw me that blind pass? Remember we're on the same team, jackass. Are you jealous that the scouts are going to be looking at me and not you?" I took a step closer to him. The team had quieted down and I could feel their eyes on us.

"Jealous of you?" Tyler snorted. "Hardly."

"You're just making a big girly fuss about nothing." Casey nodded, agreeing with Tyler.

Normally I kept my temper in check, but today I could feel it building. I was in a bad mood because my dad had been riding my ass for days and I was still pissed about missing my date with Mikayla. Their goading pushed me over the edge. I shoved Tyler with both hands. He stumbled over Casey, who was still on the ground. I watched as Casey and Tyler exchanged a look I recognized. I was prepared when they jumped me at the same time. It was two against one, but the odds didn't bother me. I'd been outnumbered before. I landed a hard punch to Tyler's gut while he connected with my jaw. My hand was inches from his face when the sound of the whistle brought me back to reality.

Coach was beyond angry. His eyes were pinched and his forehead was deeply creased. I didn't blame him. He'd just witnessed the team captains fighting each other. Coach had a "zero tolerance" policy for that sort of behavior. I knew the punishment would be harsh. I deserved it for falling into Tyler's trap. What was worse was knowing I'd let Coach down. He was more like a father to me than my own. I could see the disappointment in his eyes, hiding under the layer of anger. I'd really fucked things up this time.

"Team, line up in the end zone. You can thank your three friends later for this next drill. We're running suicides," he yelled into his megaphone.

I heard moans and groans from the rest of the team as we took our positions. This wasn't going to be easy. "Just so there are no doubts, you're all running until you puke."

Coach blew his whistle, signaling the first round. We sprinted to the 10-yard line, touched the line with our hand, and then raced back to the goal line. "Hustle," Coach shouted angrily. Without pause, he blew his whistle again. This time we ran to the 20-yard line and back. We continued running, adding ten yards each time. By the time we completed one full round of suicides, most of the team wasn't looking good. They were slowing down and everyone was sweaty and winded. I was to blame. I shouldn't have let Tyler get to me.

Coach blew his whistle again. The team moaned even louder. I had to try to make this right. The guys had suffered enough due to my stupidity. "Coach, I'll stay and run as long as you want me to. Let the other guys go. It's not their fault."

"Not a chance, Dooner. You guys win as a team, you lose as a team, and you pay for each other's mistakes as a team," Coach bellowed. He waved his arm at me. "Now, get back out there."

We were sluggishly making our way back from the 50-yard line, when I looked back and saw Tank lagging far behind. He was clutching his side and looked like he was about to throw up. His face was the strangest shade of purplish-red I'd ever seen, reminding me of a plate full of overcooked beets.

"Dooner, Tyler, and Casey, stay," Coach announced. I felt

relieved, and wondered if he'd seen the look on Tank's face too. "The rest of you can go. Practice is over. But I must warn you, just because this morning was unnecessarily rough, I won't be taking it easy on you this afternoon. You better go home and rest up. You're to be back here at three o'clock sharp and not one minute later. Do I make myself clear?"

"Yes, sir," the team responded. I could hear in their voices how angry they all were at the three of us.

"Now get on outta here, before I change my mind." He waved his hand, dismissing them.

The team slumped off the field. No one bothered to turn around to see what further punishment Coach had planned. I didn't blame them.

Coach had us line up on the end zone again. We continued with the suicide drills. I hated every second of it, but there was no way I was going down before Tyler or Casey. I'd rather drop dead than give either of them the satisfaction of beating me. Probably realizing no one was going to give up any time soon, he finally shouted, "Alright boys, bring it in."

The three of us could barely stand. Coach gave us a disgusted look. The physical punishment was over, but I sensed the worst was yet to come. I braced myself for bad news. "Do you know what it means to be part of this team?"

"Yes," we answered, our voices filled with shame.

"As it stands right now, the three of you are benched for our first game." My mouth hung open and I heard Tyler gasp. Coach ignored our distress and continued. "You should consider yourselves lucky that I'm not throwing your stupid asses off this team. You know that I have a zero tolerance policy for fighting."

"We're sorry," we mumbled in unison. I wanted to plead our case and convince him to reverse his decision, but I knew he wouldn't. Tyler and Casey also remained silent. We'd have to prove ourselves.

"What the hell were you three thinking? You're supposed

to be my dream team!" He lamented. "Go. I'm sick of looking at you." He turned and walked slowly toward the school.

I watched his retreating figure, trying to muster the strength to move. I felt frozen in place. The news was even worse than I'd imagined. Tyler and Casey also seemed to be in shock.

"I can't believe we're going to miss the biggest game of the season." I slumped my shoulders.

"It fucking sucks," Tyler agreed. I wanted to say that it was his fault we were in this predicament, but I bit my tongue.

"You can say that again," said Casey.

"I have a lot riding on that game," stated Tyler emphatically. He wasn't the only one. The scouts would be there. The scholarship was my one chance to get out of this town.

Determinedly I said, "We'll have to make sure that we change Coach's mind."

We walked silently to the locker room, each lost in our own thoughts.

I took a quick shower and left. I kept my eyes focused on the ground. I didn't need any more trouble. I was almost to the door when someone burst out of the main office and collided with me. I didn't even have to look up to know who it was. My body registered her soft curves and lavender scent. We'd only met two days ago, but it seemed like I'd known her forever. When our bodies touched, electrical currents shot through me.

"Hey, Mikayla." Taking in her beauty and charm, I instantly regretted my decision not to call her back.

"James, I'm glad I ran into you."

"You are?" I said, my voice full of surprise. "I thought you'd be mad at me for not taking you on that hike like I promised. I had to help my dad change a tractor tire." I heard how lame that sounded as soon as the words were out of my mouth.

"That's okay, it's no big deal." She shrugged.

I wondered at her nonchalant attitude. Most girls would be fuming mad. She must not be interested. I was about to try to convince her to give me a second chance when a woman with wavy brown hair and brown eyes exited the main office.

Mikayla grabbed her arm. "Mom, I want to introduce you to a friend of mine. This is James. James, this is my mom." I was thrilled to hear her call me a friend.

"Hi. Mrs.—" I put my hand out.

"Mrs. Mooney,"

"Call me Dooner. Everyone does." We politely shook hands.

Mikayla rolled her eyes. "Mom, James offered to give me a ride home." She emphasized the word James. "Is that okay? I figured you wouldn't mind since you have a meeting this afternoon." She flashed me a devilish grin.

I wasn't really sure what was going on, but I didn't care. It looked like I was getting a second chance without even having to ask. I played along. "I don't mind dropping Mikayla off." I stressed her name. "It's on my way."

"Sure, that's fine." Mrs. Mooney chuckled, apparently finding amusement in our playful banter. "I'll see you later at home."

Once we were out of earshot, I turned to Mikayla and asked, "Do you really want a ride home, or was that some sort of cover-up for your mom's benefit?" I looked back over my shoulder and saw that she'd already disappeared down the long hall. "Either way it's cool."

"I really want a ride home." She followed me out to Old Faithful. I opened the passenger door for her and she hopped in. I enjoyed what she was wearing today—faded jean shorts and a fitted red T-shirt with black Converse sneakers. Her hair was pulled back into a ponytail, curls escaping everywhere.

I walked around the truck and climbed into the driver's seat. I started the engine and headed in the direction of her grandfather's farm. The radio was on; I played with the dials, searching for a song.

Mikayla was the first to speak. "When you drop me off, do you have a sec'?"

"Yeah, I have a two hour break before I have to be back at practice." Maybe my day wasn't going to be so bad after all.

"Perfect." She didn't say anything else, but left me wondering what she had in mind. She leaned her head back and relaxed as the wind from the open window blew her hair all around. I wasn't prepared for how happy it made me feel to see her riding in my truck. I could get used to having her next to me.

I waited until we were parked in her driveway to apologize. I cleared my throat. "I'm sorry about yesterday. Thanks for giving me a second chance. What can I do to make it up to you?"

"You just did by giving me a ride home. We can call it even." She smiled. "Wait here. I'll be right back." She quickly jumped down from the truck and walked toward the house.

Without even being invited, I followed her.

She stopped on the front porch and turned around to face me, "Wait here. And I mean it." She pointed her finger at my chest.

"Where are you going?" I asked, but she didn't respond.

She disappeared into the house, returning a minute later. "Here's your shirt. I washed it for you." She held it out to me.

I was taken aback. This was not what I had expected. "I said you could keep it." I pushed it back at her.

"You said a lot of things." She sounded both angry and hurt.

Finally I understood why she had me drive her home. She wasn't giving me a second chance; she was paying me back for standing her up. She led me here on false pretenses only to let me down. "So you are mad about yesterday." She didn't say anything but the angry look on her face said it all. "I really was helping my dad change a tractor tire. I called. Didn't Emma tell you?"

"Yeah and she also said that you'd call back."

"I took a shower and then crashed." I didn't tell her that until I ran into her today I'd decided she'd be better off without me. "Changing a tractor tire isn't as easy as it sounds." I took a deep breath. Lowering my voice and changing my tone, I added, "I'm sorry I didn't call. Can you give me another chance?"

"No." She turned to disappear back into the house.

I couldn't let her go that easy. I had to get her to change her mind about me. I reached out and quickly pulled her against my chest. I could feel her heart beating against mine. I paused one second too long the other night and I wasn't about to make the same mistake twice. I dipped my head down. I couldn't wait to taste the sweetness of her mouth. I was inches away from touching my lips to hers when she stiffened in my arms.

She pushed against my chest with both hands. I let her go. "It's time for you to leave, James." She stormed inside, slamming the door behind her.

I bent over and picked up my fallen shirt. I left it neatly folded on the swing. I wanted her, but I could wait. Forcing her to feel something that she wasn't ready for was not my style. She'd come around. She wouldn't have bothered to go to such extremes to get back at me if she didn't care. I'd give her time to cool down and then I'd be back.

Chapter Nine

Mike

I banged the kitchen cupboard doors, releasing frustration. I rummaged around in the refrigerator, searching for something to eat—I tended to eat when I was upset. Due to a lack of better options, I decided on a peanut butter and jelly sandwich. I slammed the ingredients down on the counter. Slapping two pieces of bread together, I made a quick sandwich. I added a handful of chips to my plate.

Pop-Pop strolled into the kitchen. "What's all the ruckus? It feels like an earthquake. I know you miss California and all, but this is taking it too far."

"I'm making lunch," I retorted as I plopped down at the table to eat.

"What you got there?" he asked, eyeing my sandwich.

"Plain old pb and j."

"All that noise just to make a peanut butter and jelly sandwich?" Pop-Pop settled into his usual place at the kitchen table, folding his hands. Silently he watched as I stuffed a handful of salty chips in my mouth and chewed. I felt guilty for eating in front of him. "Do you want me to make you one?" I mumbled with my mouth full.

"I don't eat peanut butter. I can't stand the stuff. I never could understand why kids love it so much."

"It's good." I took a bite of my sandwich and acted like I was eating a fifty-dollar lobster tail.

"I'll take your word for it. What I'd love is a turkey sandwich with some homegrown lettuce on it. A slice of tomato would taste good too."

I scraped my chair loudly across the kitchen floor as I pushed back from the table. Once again I rummaged around, getting out all the ingredients. Only this time I made a turkey sandwich.

"You sure are like a bull in a china shop," he snickered.

My heart softened a little. My dad used to tell me that.

I'd almost finished making his lunch when he added, "Oh yeah, don't forget the dill pickle. I like a dill pickle on the side. And no chips for me."

"No problem," I muttered, doing what he'd requested. I placed the plate in front of him.

"Thanks," he said, taking a big bite. "Not bad. Not bad at all."

I sat back down to finish my own lunch.

"Did you see Emma at school?"

"Nope."

"Didn't she have cheerleading try-outs today?"

"I think so." I didn't pay much attention to what Emma did.

"I wonder if she made the squad. She sure seemed excited. It's good to see her trying to make friends" He was speaking more to himself than to me. "For her sake, I hope she makes the team. What's your story? You make any friends yet?"

"I already have friends. Too bad they're all on the West Coast."

"Humph." He crunched into his pickle, ignoring my surly attitude. "What about that truck I saw pull out of my driveway a few minutes ago? I thought I recognized it. Doesn't it belong to Jack Muldoon's son? I can't remember the boy's first name." He scratched his head. "What I do know is that he's one hell of a football player. Why, he's even got a shot at playing pro ball. Imagine, a farmer's kid with all that talent. Just goes to show you that you can't judge a book by its cover."

"You and your clichés," I exclaimed, letting out a deep sigh. "Now I know where Aunt Carol gets them."

"What's wrong with them?" he asked.

"Really, Pops," I said, giving him a nickname. It suited him better than Pop-Pop. I could tell he thought so too. His eyes brightened.

Turning serious again, he said, "You didn't answer my question. Is that Muldoon boy a friend of yours?"

"His name is James. Most call him Dooner." I rolled my eyes to indicate how ridiculous his nickname sounded. "Either way, I'd hardly call him a friend. We just met three days ago."

"Well, I saw how that boy looked at you, and to me it looked like he's interested in being more than your friend. I may be old, but I can recognize when a boy wants to court a girl."

"Excuse me?" I shook my head. "Do you know what year it is? People don't use the word 'court' anymore." Once I got beyond the old fashioned vocabulary, I realized that he must have been watching us. My face turned red. "You were spying on us?"

"I wasn't spying on you. I was sitting in my chair, working on today's crossword puzzle, like always. I heard a truck pull in, so I got up to see who it was. The two of you were talking on the porch. It was nothing that concerned me, so I sat back down."

I scowled.

"That reminds me. Today's puzzle's a tough one. Maybe you can help. Your mom's always going on about how smart you are." He pulled the crossword out of his front shirt pocket. "Do you know the Spanish word for bear?"

"Oso. O-s-o," I readily responded.

He clicked his pen and filled in the answer. "By golly, Miss Molly, you're right. It fits."

I shook my head in disbelief at how easily he'd succeeded in distracting me. "Good one, trying to make me forget that we were talking about you spying on me." He looked baffled, but Pops was sharper than he was pretending to be. "As I was saying, I don't know what you saw, but James is not my friend."

He raised one eyebrow. "Why not give him a chance? I'm sure he's a nice fellow."

I put it in terms he'd understand. "Let's just say, I can't believe they make a helmet big enough to fit his big head!"

Pops laughed heartily. I found myself joining him. "Now you're catching on."

Pops continued to ask me crossword puzzle questions while we finished lunch. I discovered I knew more trivia than I thought; I was actually enjoying myself. In no time, the puzzle was complete. I carried the plates to the sink and loaded them into the dishwasher. Pops should recommend that Aunt Carol get one.

"Thanks for lunch and for cleaning up too." He smiled. Maybe he did need us here. "I'm going back to my chair. I have to a find a new puzzle to work on."

"Okay." I had to find something to occupy my time this afternoon.

I was about to go upstairs when he called, "Mike?"

"Yeah?" I peeped my head into the living room.

"Just so you know, Tyler and your new friend don't get along." Why was he telling me this? It seemed out of character. Pops didn't strike me as someone who gossiped or meddled in other people's business.

"Okay?" I waited for him to continue.

"Tyler likes to cause mischief for him." He gave me a look as if to say that perhaps James could use my help. What was it with Pops and this guy?

"I'm sure James can take care of himself. He's a big boy," I stated, recalling his broad frame and towering height.

"He's a good kid. Tyler gives him grief, and so does his own father. All I'm saying is maybe next time you could be a little nicer to him. You could invite him in."

"Why would I do that?" I asked incredulously.

"I don't know. It seems to me that both of you could use a friend." He turned his attention to the puzzle in his hand.

"What exactly did you mean about his father?" I thought back to the excuse that James gave for blowing me off the other day. He said it was because he was too busy helping his dad. Was there more to it than that?

"Nothing." He kept his eyes down, mumbling something about number twenty-two down. I stood in front of him and grabbed his pen off the table. I tapped it against my palm.

"Mike, don't be difficult now. Hand me my pen." He held out his hand.

I placed the pen behind my ear and put my hands on my hips, "Not until you tell me exactly what you meant."

"I can go and get another pen."

"You can, but you won't."

"Let's just say that in a small town you hear things, even when you're not listening."

"Like what?"

H took a deep breath and sighed. "It's a terrible thing that your daddy died, but at least you know that he loved you." He folded his arms across his big chest, signaling that the conversation was over. "Now, give me that pen." He reached up and snatched it from behind my ear, filling in another answer.

I slowly climbed the stairs to my room. Flopping down on my bed, I replayed the conversation with Pops. I tried to make sense out if it, but I couldn't. It was like trying to solve a crossword puzzle with only partial clues. I felt frustrated.

Suddenly I knew how to pass the afternoon. Drawing always calmed me. When I pulled images from my mind and put them on paper it helped me make sense of the world. I stood up and began searching the room for my backpack. I finally found it hiding under a pile of Emma's dirty clothes. I quickly filled it with art supplies, tossed in a sketchpad and a box filled with my favorite drawing pencils.

I tore back down the stairs, anxious to get started. "I'm going for a walk. I'll be back in a while," I called out as I left.

I crossed the main road and entered the cemetery that had been beckoning me since we first arrived. In all of my visits I'd never set foot here. I walked around, examining the tombstones and running my hands over them. Some were crumbling and moss-covered. I brushed one off to see the name and date. Then I brushed off another and another. Some dated as far back as 1832. I stared across the street at my grandparents' old farmhouse. According to the names on the graves and the close proximity to the farm, I concluded that all the people buried here were relatives.

I sat down with my back against the giant oak tree. Pulling out my sketchpad and pencils, I sketched the tombstone in front of me. I felt the pain of having recently lost my dad. A tear rolled down my cheek and I quickly brushed it away with the back of my hand. I wasn't usually an emotional person.

I didn't think while I drew. The pencil flew across the page making marks, almost as if it had a mind of its own. Often times I didn't know what it was going to be until it was completed. The cemetery was still with only a few birds calling off in the distance from time to time. When I finished I was not at all surprised by what had taken form on my paper. It was a portrait of my dad. He was sitting behind the tombstone, using it as a desk, his laptop open in front of him. He wore a peaceful smile. I smiled, too, as another tear fell. I realized I'd dreaded moving here because I thought I'd feel so far away from my dad and the life we'd all had together in California.

Now I knew that was silly. He was always with me, even here in the middle of Nowhere. It didn't matter where we lived. My father had loved me and he lived on in my memories. I shut my notepad, feeling better than I had in months.

Chapter Ten

Dooner

Practice was hell all week. Stepping under the scalding hot shower in the locker room, I washed away a full day's worth of sweat and dirt. The week had started off bad when I let Tyler and Casey coerce me into starting a fight, and since then nothing had improved. I was still being benched for the season's opener. I had to do something—and fast—to change that. I mulled a plan over in my mind as I lathered shampoo into my hair. I'd do whatever it took to make sure that I played in that game. I rinsed my hair and then abruptly turned off the shower. Grabbing my towel, I quickly dried off. It was time I had a talk with Tyler and Casey.

"Tyler, we need to talk." He was just changing out of his shoulder pads. "Tell your buddy, Casey, to join us too."

"Sure," he grunted.

"Meet me outside when you guys are done getting dressed."

"Sure," he grunted a second time.

I quickly pulled on a clean pair of jeans and a T-shirt. It never took me more than a few minutes to get ready. I went outside to wait for them.

A few minutes later Tyler and Casey emerged from the school. I got right down to business, "We need to stop acting like enemies. We have to put our differences aside and do what's right for this team." Tyler mumbled his consent. I continued my pep talk. "This is our senior year, the year we've been waiting for. I don't know about you, but I don't want to be on the sidelines acting as a bench warmer. I want to be playing in the game, leading the team to its fiftieth straight win." I pounded my fist into my palm.

"Me too," agreed Tyler. Getting Tyler to work with me, instead of against me, was going better than I could have hoped.

"I don't know why you intentionally threw me that blind pass." I looked angrily at Tyler. "And why you," I said, shifting my gaze to glare at Casey, "slammed into me so hard, but I'm willing to put it behind me." I swallowed to push back the bile that was threatening to rise. I hated giving in like this, but I couldn't miss that game. "As long as you promise not to try anything like that again. We need to move on and work together."

"I agree," said Tyler.

Casey nodded.

"I'll pretend it never happened on one condition," amended Tyler.

"I'm not playing games with you, man. This is serious." I scowled.

"So is this. Stay away from my cousin, Mike."

"Mikayla...What does she have to do with anything?"

"Just stay away from her. She's been through a lot already and she doesn't need a guy like you trying to get in her pants."

"I'm not trying to get in her pants," I declared, outraged. I wasn't a perfect angel, but unlike the rest of the guys on the team, I didn't go round trying to bang every skirt I saw.

"I mean it. Stay away from her."

"I can't promise that." I smiled as I remembered how soft

she felt in my arms. I'd been biding my time this week until I could stop by and see her.

"Then there's no deal." He turned to leave.

"I don't understand," I called out unwilling to let Tyler leave.

He turned back around, "What?"

"You didn't seem to have a problem the other night when you left it to me to make sure her and her sister got home okay."

Tyler shifted uncomfortably. "Yeah, that was a bad decision on my part."

"They made it home safe, right?"

"Yeah, they did," he grumpily admitted.

"Okay, then. I think worrying about whom your cousin dates is the least of your problems. Mikayla seems like she's going to do whatever she wants regardless of what you say, anyway." Tyler grimaced, probably recalling how he couldn't talk her out of walking home. "Can we please get back to playing football now?" I pleaded.

For once Tyler kept his mouth shut and looked ready to listen. Casey stood by his side.

I filled them in on my plan. It was especially important that, going forward, Coach saw Tyler and me connecting on the field and in the locker room. As the team captains, we set the tone.

We planned to meet every morning before practice to run drills, throwing the ball with Casey playing defense. Almost all of our opponents ran the ball; either they didn't have a quarterback with a strong enough arm to throw down field, or they lacked a receiver who could catch it. Lucky for us, we had both. We were going to surprise everyone by perfecting our passing game. When Coach saw how serious we were, he'd change his mind about suspending us.

"Monday morning at seven?" I asked, looking at them.

"I'll be here," said Tyler.

"Me too." Casey nodded.

There was a lightness in my step as I walked to where I'd parked Old Faithful. I quickly threw my gym bag in the back and started her up. I was in a hurry to get to where I was going before my luck changed.

Chapter Eleven

Mike

I'd been procrastinating since I woke up. I wasn't dressed, even though it was after noon. I was lounging on my bed in my pajamas, my hair carelessly pulled back into a ponytail, while I sketched the view from my bedroom window. It was an aerial view of the cemetery.

"Mike," Pops yelled up the stairs.

"What?" I yelled back.

"Come on down here."

I looked at the clock and saw that it was almost twelve-thirty. I'd been making lunch all week and he was probably hungry. Come to think of it, I was hungry too. "Okay. I'll be down in a sec." I stood and stretched. I thought about getting dressed, but I didn't really see the point. I wasn't going anywhere and Pops couldn't have cared less about fashion.

"Stop your stalling and get down here. You've slept half the day away already."

"Coming," I shouted, stomping loudly down the stairs in an attempt to annoy Pops. He hated it when I walked like an elephant. "Here I am, Pops." I raised my right hand and saluted. "Reporting for duty."

He chuckled good-naturedly and I felt my heart soften. Like my dad, he actually understood and even appreciated my humor. Suddenly I felt bad for making so much noise when I came down the stairs.

Pops kept his voice low and pointed toward the kitchen, "You have a visitor."

"A visitor?" Surprise filled my voice. *I couldn't imagine who it could be.* Paige wouldn't be here for a couple of weeks. She was coming to visit for my birthday. "Who is it?" I whispered.

"So you do know how to be quiet." He smiled, ignoring my question completely.

I rolled my eyes. "Pops! Who's here?" I repeated just as James came out of the kitchen. My mouth fell to the floor. He was the last person I'd expected to see. I think I would have been less shocked if my dad had walked into the room.

"Hi," he said, a huge smile spreading across his handsome face. I almost forgot myself as I stared into his bright green eyes. I wasn't sure how long I'd been staring, but when Pops cleared his throat, I snapped out of it.

"What are you doing here?" I asked through gritted teeth. I quickly crossed my arms over my chest, suddenly remembering I was wearing pajamas and no bra.

"I have the afternoon free. I thought maybe we could take that hike now."

"So you just show up, assuming that I'd drop what I was doing and go on a hike with you." My voice rose an octave.

"I can see you've been busy." James nodded at my outfit and Pops laughed. I shot him a dark look to let him know I didn't appreciate him taking James's side in any of this.

"I've been—" I was trying to think of a logical excuse for still being in my pajamas, when Pop-Pop interrupted.

"If you don't want to go, you can help me in the garden. It needs some attention. There are weeds to pull, plants to water, and vegetables to pick for the stand. I was waiting for you to help me replenish our supply and empty the cash box. If you'd rather stay home, you can always help me." He grinned.

I couldn't believe the nerve of my own grandfather, trying to set me up. He knew I loathed gardening. I glared at the two of them. I felt like I was being backed into a corner and there was no way out.

"I need a few minutes to get ready," I grumbled in defeat.

"Take your time. I'm not in a hurry."

"James can keep me company," Pops spoke up. "I have a few crossword puzzle questions that I couldn't answer because someone was too busy this morning to help." I watched as Pop led James toward the kitchen. He was already pulling the puzzle out of his front pocket. "Are you any good at puzzles?"

I sighed and raced up the stairs two at a time. I didn't want them talking and comparing notes about me.

I slammed my door, rattling the windows. I dashed around my room, gathering my strewn clothes. I didn't know what to wear for a hike. I'd noticed that James wore torn jeans, a T-shirt and sneakers. I wondered if he had on jeans because there'd be branches to scratch up his legs, or if he always wore them. I'd never seen him in anything else. Quickly, I pulled on a clean pair of jean shorts and a turquoise T-shirt. I ran into the bathroom. In record time I washed my face, brushed my teeth, and redid my ponytail. I'd been gone ten minutes, tops. As I raced back down the stairs, Pop-pop's laughter filled the air. *Oh, no. This can't be good.*

"What's going on?" I asked, sounding out of breath.

"Your grandfather suggested I use some of these tomatoes," James explained, holding up a large ripe beefsteak, "to make sandwiches to bring along on our hike."

"Great idea," I said, faking a smile. I was going to have a talk with Pops later.

"Here's one for you too." He handed Pops a paper towel with a delicious looking tomato sandwich on it.

I rolled my eyes. "I see that his suggestion was self-serving."

"Of course. It's lunchtime, you know. You were too busy to make an old guy a sandwich." Pops took a big bite and then wiped his mouth with a napkin. "It's good. If it makes you feel any better, it doesn't taste as good as yours." He winked at me.

I huffed and put my hands on my hips.

"Do you have something we can carry these in?" James politely asked me while holding four huge sandwiches. I'd been starring angrily at Pops for so long that I'd almost forgotten James and our own picnic.

"Who are all those sandwiches for?" I looked around the kitchen to see if someone else was joining us. It would be just like Emma to show up and invite herself along. But I didn't see her.

"No, it's just us. I'm hungry." James' green eyes deepened. Suddenly he seemed shy and embarrassed. Seeing him humbled, warmed my heart. He shrugged. "I have a big appetite." I smiled in spite of myself. He certainly didn't look like his appetite was too big; there wasn't an ounce of fat on him. His muscles were perfectly toned. I knew first-hand that he had a perfect washboard stomach hiding out under his T-shirt. It was my turn to blush.

I needed a distraction. I began to look for my backpack to carry the sandwiches. I didn't want James to see the affect he had on me. I was like an elementary school girl having my first crush.

"Here, we can use this to carry everything," I said, locating my backpack hanging on a peg by the door,

"Perfect." James added the sandwiches, water bottles, and apples, to the backpack while I held it open. Our hands lightly brushed and I almost dropped everything when an electrical shock traveled up my arm and throughout my body. I looked up and James was wearing a surprised but pleased look that matched my own.

He was the first to speak. "I think we're all set."

I took a deep breath to calm my nerves. "Okay."

"Have fun you two," Pop-pop wished us as we left through the back door.

As soon as we were outside and beyond hearing range, I gave James a piece of my mind. Mostly I was angry because I felt things I couldn't explain, but I wasn't about to admit it. "How dare you just show up here without calling?" My face flushed as I recalled how stupid I must have looked, standing there in my PJ's. "And worse, how dare you use my own grandfather against me?"

He laughed, showing off deep dimples. "Your grandfather's quite a character. He's an ally I hadn't counted on."

"Hmph." I walked a couple of steps ahead although I had no idea which direction we were headed in.

"I was surprised how eager he seemed to get rid of you today," he teased, catching up to me.

"I know, right? As if I don't help him every day with his precious tomato plants," I mumbled, hurt. Pops and I'd been spending a lot of time together and I thought we enjoyed each other's company.

"I was only joking." Turning serious, he explained, "I only meant that he seemed happy to see you getting out of the house. I think he worries about you. He wants you to be happy here."

James was right. Pops was only looking out for me. "He must've been a match-maker in a previous life," I said, lightening the mood.

James grinned. "I bet he was a good one."

"We'll see." I shrugged. I didn't want him to think he was completely forgiven for showing up unannounced. "This date didn't exactly start off on the right foot." *Did I really just say that?* I do need to get out of the house more. Pop-pop's clichés are rubbing off on me.

"I honestly didn't think you'd mind me stopping by. I

thought you thrived on spontaneity." James winked.

"Yeah, but not when I'm still in my pajamas." I laughed, realizing how ridiculous I must have looked, standing in the front hallway wearing my Hello Kitty tank top and pink boxer-like pajama shorts.

James laughed too until I slapped him playfully on the arm, signaling him to knock it off.

We crossed the main road and entered the cornfield. The corn was tall, even taller than James. I hoped he knew where he was going because it all looked the same to me. We walked for several minutes and the only sound was rustling stalks. I was about to ask him if we were lost, when we finally came to the edge of the field.

"Here's the trail I told you about." He pointed to a dirt path about two and half feet wide that cut through the woods. "It's about a mile walk to the creek, which then empties into a deep pond. That would be a great place to stop and eat our lunch."

"Lead the way." I followed along behind; the trail wasn't wide enough for the two of us. He held branches out of the way, acting as a kind-hearted guide. I paid little attention to the luscious green surroundings—I was too busy enjoying the view of James' broad backside. We walked in comfortable silence. I listened to the sounds of animals scurrying and birds tweeting.

"Have you taken this trail before?" I asked, my curiosity getting the better of me.

"Yes."

"Have you taken this trail with other girls?" I hadn't meant to ask that out loud, but I had a habit of saying whatever was on my mind. I didn't want to come across as a jealous girlfriend, because I wasn't, but this place felt intimate and special and secretly I wanted to be the only one he'd shown it to.

He laughed. It was a hearty laugh, but it sounded rough

and raspy, like he didn't laugh often enough. When he calmed, he turned around to face me. His dimples showed prominently, momentarily stopping my heart. "No. Why?"

"Just wondered." I couldn't hide my smile at hearing the answer I wanted.

"I've always come here alone. It's a great place to clear my mind and think. I never wanted to show this place to anyone, until now."

"Really?" I questioned.

"Really."

"Why me?"

"I like you. You seem different than the girls around here." It wasn't a long explanation, but it was all I needed. Soon the trail widened and he reached for my hand, and I welcomed the feel of his strong hand in mine. A rush of heat flowed through me,

Wanting to get to know him better, I asked, "Have you lived here your whole life?"

"Yes." His one-word answers were beginning to frustrate me. How was I supposed to get to know him if he didn't ever elaborate?

"Do you like living here in such a small town?"

"It has its advantages and disadvantages."

"Like what?"

He didn't answer my question, instead turning it around. "Did you like growing up in a big city?"

"It had its advantages and disadvantages." Two could play at this game.

"Touché." He laughed. My heart warmed at having made him laugh again.

I heard the creek bubbling before I could see it. I loved the relaxing sound of water rushing over rocks. It turned out to be a small creek with scraggly trees lining the banks. It appeared to be ankle deep with crystal clear water. I could see rocks and small stones lining the bottom.

"Do you want to walk in it for a while?" He asked, and I grinned, instantly liking the idea. "I have to warn you that it's cold, but not too cold."

"I'm not afraid of a little cold water."

"Excellent." He nodded. "It gets deeper and picks up speed a little further down just before it empties into the pond. We can rest there and eat our lunch on the big boulders."

"Sounds like a plan." I was hot and the idea of wading in the cool water appealed to me. I let go of his hand and bent down to untie my sneakers.

"Leave 'em on. The rocks on the bottom are sharp. You don't want to cut your foot. Also, it'll be easier to walk on the slippery rocks."

"Oh, okay." I felt like a silly city girl.

James rolled up his jeans and stepped down into the creek. He held his hand out to help me down the slight bank. We continued to hold hands as we waded through the cold water. It was a good thing, too, because several times I gripped his hand tighter to avoid falling. Normally I wasn't so clumsy; I think it had to do with being near James. He was confident and sure of every step he took. Except for the babble of the creek and the splashing of our footsteps, it was quiet and peaceful. I didn't ask James any more questions. Talking right now would have been intrusive.

Once the creek picked up speed, we climbed out and walked on the trail. A surprisingly large waterfall cascaded over big boulders and emptied into a pond. We stopped, and I marveled that such a beautiful oasis existed here in Nowhere. The pond was just as clear as the creek had been. It looked to be eight or nine feet deep. The woods were on one bank, while large boulders sat on the other.

"James, this is amazing." I couldn't find the right words to express how beautiful this place was, or how happy I was that he'd brought me here. I smiled sincerely. "Thanks."

"You're welcome." He reached out and tucked a curl

behind my ear.

We stared into each other's eyes and time seemed to stand still. I thought he was going to kiss me, when his stomach growled loudly. We laughed at the same time.

"Let's eat lunch," I announced in response to his rumbling stomach.

We sat on a large boulder in the sun. Opening my backpack, I handed him a sandwich. I ate one to James' three. We chatted while we ate and for the first time all day James gave more than one word answers. The pond provided the perfect setting. I felt relaxed and free to be myself.

He patted his stomach. "That was great." I laughed at his enthusiasm.

"Is it safe to swim in the pond?" I asked, eyeing it longingly. It looked so inviting.

"You would swim in it?" He sounded skeptical.

"Of course." I lifted my ponytail off the back of my neck. The humidity made my hair curlier and messier yet. "It would be so refreshing. I'm used to a dry heat."

"Awesome." His dimples showed again.

"Is it safe?"

"Yes."

That was all I needed to hear. I quickly stood up and stripped down to my bra and underwear, while James appeared rooted to the spot. I heard him suck in his breath. Tossing my clothes on the rock, I jumped into the bone-chilling water. There was no other way to get into water this cold. I stayed under, holding my breath for as long as I could. I resurfaced, laughing.

I wiped the water from my eyes and saw James scowl.

"What the hell, Mikayla?" he shouted upset. "You scared the shit out of me."

"I'm sorry," I quickly apologized. "I didn't mean to scare you. I was only trying to have a little fun." I trembled, thinking how close I'd come to ruining our perfect afternoon.

Sternly, he said, "You have to promise not to do anything like that again."

"I promise." I made a show of crossing my heart.

He nodded, accepting my apology.

"You should join me," I said, grinning wickedly. I splashed at the water, soaking him.

He didn't waste time. He quickly pulled off his shirt and unzipped his jeans. He was wearing black boxer briefs that fit him just right. He was so beautiful that he could have been the next Calvin Klein underwear model. He took several big steps backwards, then ran and jumped into the pond, holding his legs with his arms, cannon-ball style. A huge splash erupted, hitting me full in the face.

"Did I splash you?" he asked innocently, as I wiped water out of my eyes.

"Yes." I splashed him back. We both laughed.

We goofed around, splashing and showing off. We made a contest out of jumping off the ledge and rating the biggest splashes. Of course, James won every time. Then we raced each other from one edge to the other, which was something I was good at because at one time I had been on a summer league swim team. I hadn't laughed so much in months. I didn't want this moment to ever end. I wasn't sure how much time had passed until teeth began to chatter, signaling we'd been at it awhile.

"Your lips are purple," James declared, swimming over to my side and lightly touching my lips with his fingertip. My breath caught in my throat.

"I don't want to get out," I admitted, visibly shaking.

"Come on, we'll warm up in the sun." He strode over to the large boulder in the sun and lay down on his back, his hands folded underneath his head. Feeling shy all of a sudden, I lay down next to him without touching. I didn't know if I was ready to get that close to him yet. It had been a perfect afternoon and I didn't want to ruin it by feeling too much, and

I knew being that close to James would make me feel things I'd never even come close to feeling before. However even with the warm sun soaking into my skin, I shook. My skin was covered in goose bumps.

"Here," without hesitating, he pulled me against him and tucked me underneath his arm, "I'll warm you up."

Being close to him, I warmed instantly, and my worries vanished. It felt right being in his arms. I relaxed and rested my head on his perfectly chiseled chest.

The swim, the sun, and the strong arm wrapped around me, equaled perfect harmony. In fact I was so comfortable that I was having a hard time keeping my eyes open. I drifted off to sleep.

"I had fun today," someone whispered in my ear.

I recognized the husky voice, even in my dreams—James' voice. It was such a wonderful dream that I didn't want to wake up. I groggily shifted to brush my hair out of my face. I gasped when I touched hard muscle that was too real to be part of a dream. I quickly sat up and wrapped my arms around my knees, feeling self-conscious. I was still wearing only my bra and underwear. "I'm sorry I fell asleep."

"Don't worry about it. It was nice holding you." He sat up. His green eyes practically sparkled in the sunlight. He pulled a curl and absentmindedly twirled it around his finger

I couldn't move. I focused on breathing—in and out. It was difficult to form a single thought while sitting so close to him. My mind was telling me to get dressed and yet my heart was telling me to stay where I was. Quietly I said, "I had a great time today. I felt so safe, so right, in your arms." He continued to twirl my hair. I rarely shared things about myself, but today I wanted to. I added, "I haven't been sleeping well since my dad died unexpectedly, over six months ago. I'm lucky if I can fall asleep at all, and when I do I never sleep for more than an hour or two at a time."

James took my hand in his. "I'm happy that you feel so

comfortable with me. I feel the same way about you, like a part of me has always known you, even though we just met." He brought my hand to his lips and lightly kissed it. "I'm sorry about your dad. Were you close to him?"

"Yes. He understood me when no one else did." I gazed into his kind eyes. They were a clear, bright green color. I took a deep breath and continued. "We had a big fight the morning of the day he died. I'd come down the stairs wearing a really short skirt and a tight blue T-shirt. I knew it wasn't something I should wear to school, but I didn't care. It was the first thing I saw so I pulled it on. I was running late, like always. My dad threw a fit and refused to let me leave the house. I argued with him, saying some pretty awful things. I was pissed at him for making me change. I stormed out of the house, refusing to acknowledge him when he called out to me. I was in the worst mood all morning at school. I felt horrible about my temper tantrum and the mean things I'd shouted at my dad. I was going to apologize later that evening. Only I never got the chance. Just after lunch I was called down to the office. I took my time, thinking for sure it was in reference to my short skirt. The principal instructed me to sit down, and I could tell by the somber look on his face that it had nothing to do with what I was wearing. He carefully explained how my dad had suffered a heart attack and was in the hospital. A taxi came to pick me up and I rode in stunned silence to meet my mom and Emma, who were already at the hospital. Emma had stayed home from school with a headache. The traffic on the freeway was especially bad that afternoon and by the time I arrived, it was too late. He'd died. There was nothing they could do. I've always thought that if only I hadn't argued with him, maybe his blood pressure wouldn't have skyrocketed, and he wouldn't have died."

James gently wiped tears off my cheeks. I didn't even know I was crying. "It's not your fault, you know."

Deep down inside, I knew it wasn't, but it was easy to

blame myself anyway. Talking to James made some of the built-up guilt and anger disappear. It helped me to finally see things clearly. Slowly I nodded, "I know. He had a degenerate heart condition that no one knew about until it was too late."

"I'm sorry you've had to go through all of this. I can't imagine it's been easy." He squeezed my hand.

"It's been hard on all of us. I'm mad at my dad for dying and leaving us, but I take it out on my mom. She's the only one here. I haven't been very nice to her." I hadn't realized how true that was until now. Gaining confidence, I added. "You wouldn't believe the fit I threw about moving here."

"What about now, are you still upset that you moved here?"

Staring at James' handsome face, it was hard to be too upset. "I might be coming around, a little," I confessed.

"Well, I'm glad that you did." As if to prove it, he slowly leaned in and pressed his lips firmly against mine. I responded by passionately kissing him back. Our tongues lightly teased one another's.

He pulled away, "What about now, are you happy yet?"

"Almost," I smirked.

James took the hint and kissed me again, I lay down on my back while he leaned over me with his hands on either side of my head. Our kisses were demanding and urgent. I ran my hands through his hair and down his muscular back. Our breathing came in gasps.

"Happy yet?" He asked, rolling onto his side. Before I could answer, he began kissing my neck. I had no idea that having my neck kissed could cause sparks in other places.

"Yeah, I'm happy." I laughed as his tongue tickled me behind my ear.

His kisses made a trail down my neck. Suddenly, he pushed my bra strap down and gently kissed my nipple. Surprised, I pulled away and sat up. "This is moving too fast." My face flushed. "I don't want to be a tease, but I'm not ready to have sex. I'm not the kind of girl who sleeps with a boy on the first date." To keep the moment from getting awkward I added, "Even if he does get extra points for taking her to their own private swimming hole."

He sat up too. "I'm sorry." Almost under his breath he muttered, "Damn, I told myself not to get carried away."

"It's okay." I laid my hand on his arm. "I just wanted to be honest with you. It's not that I'm a virgin, exactly. I had sex once before, but it wasn't what I expected. I did it because I wanted to find out why everyone always went on and on about how great sex was. Only it wasn't all that great for me. My big mistake was that I wasn't in love with him and he wasn't in love with me. At the time, I thought it didn't matter. I thought it would be okay, but it wasn't. It was painful. It was nothing like the heartfelt lovemaking I read about in romance novels or saw in movies." I should've been embarrassed to confess all of this to James, but I wasn't. I marveled at how easy it was to talk to him. When I looked into his clear green eyes, I wanted to tell him things I'd never told anyone. "Technically I'm not a virgin, but I still feel like one. I made a promise to myself that when I have sex again, it will be for all the right reasons. It will because I'm in love. I know it probably sounds stupid to you, but I want the fairytale."

He nodded. "It doesn't sound stupid to me. And if anyone deserves the fairytale ending, it's you. I'm sorry I got so carried away. It felt so damn good to hold you in my arms and kiss you. But that's no excuse." He held my face in his hands, "I promise to be more in charge of my hormones from now on. I want you to know that I would never do anything to hurt you."

"I know you wouldn't." I couldn't imagine James hurting anyone. He appeared tough on the outside, but it was all an act.

He let go of my face, but continued to look me in the eye. "I also want you to know that I'm sorry I didn't call you when I said I would. It's sort of a long story, but long story short, my dad can be a pain in the ass. Last Sunday he kept me busy all day until I was so tired that I crashed." I noticed that his green eyes turned cloudy when he mentioned his dad. "Thanks for giving me a second chance." His eyes were bright once again.

"My pleasure." I smiled, remembering how his kisses made my heart race. It would be easy to get carried away again. "Maybe we should get dressed now."

"Good idea." He put out his hand and helped me to my feet. We each located our long-ago discarded clothes. Turning our backs to one other, we quickly got dressed.

"Are you still happy that you moved here?" He turned to face me, his brow furrowed with concern.

"Of course." I reached for his hand.

"Are you sure I didn't mess things up between us?"

"I'm sure." I smiled. Pushing up on my tip-toes, I gently planted a kiss on his lips.

"We should head back." He stroked my hair. "We've been gone a long time."

"Okay." I nodded in agreement. I reached down and picked up the backpack that we'd used to carry the picnic. We walked along the creek holding hands. My step was lighter than it had been earlier.

Small talk had never interested me before, so I was surprised by my desire to ask him seemingly trivial questions. "What's your favorite color?"

"Orange."

"What's your favorite food?"

He smirked, showing off his dimples. "Country fried steak and eggs."

"What's your favorite class?"

He chuckled. "What is this, twenty questions?"

"Sort of." I shrugged. "I want to get to know you better."

His dimples deepened. My heart melted. "Okay. It's my turn, though. You've already asked me two questions."

"Sure. What to you want to know?"

"What's your favorite color?"

"Black and white and all the shades of gray."

"That's more than one."

"I know."

He laughed. "Why those colors?"

"I believe color can sometimes distract from something's true beauty. That's why I prefer to draw with charcoal."

"You're an artist?"

"That's three questions," I stated. I saw he really wanted me to answer so I said, "Yes. Drawing is my passion. It's my escape. It's what I do."

"I'd love to see your work sometime."

"My turn," I declared. "What's your favorite sport?" I was pretty sure it was football, but I wanted to hear it from him.

"Football." His green eyes brightened.

"What position do you play?"

"I play tight end." I furrowed my forehead. I didn't know anything about football. He continued. "It's an offensive position. I can either block or receive the ball. It's like wearing two hats." He shyly added, "Of course, my favorite is catching the ball and running it for a touchdown. Tyler and I are working on our passing game."

I smiled. I didn't really understand what James was talking about, but it was great to see this side of him. Football was important to him. I would have to have Pops explain the game to me. "I'll have to come to one of your games."

"I'd like that." He smiled brightly. His face was even more handsome when he smiled.

All too soon, we'd arrived at the edge of the cornfield. We'd be back at the farm in a few minutes. "Okay. We have time for one more question each. It's your turn," I said as we made our way through the maze.

"Where's the strangest place you've ever been kissed?" It sounded more like a dare than a question.

Playing along, I said, "In a cornfield." I stopped and faced him. Wrapping my arms around his neck, I pulled his head down to mine. The kiss started off light and quickly deepened. He pulled me closer and I could feel his heart beating against mine. My fingers played with his hair, while his were tangled in the belt loops of my jean shorts. His mouth tasted sweet and tangy. Suddenly a crow cawed overhead and we pulled away laughing.

"I was hoping you were going to say that."

"I know." It was amazing to me that in such a short amount of time we could read each other's minds.

We crossed the street and once again we were back at the farm. I had one last question. "Do you want to come in?" I asked nervously.

"I wish I could, but I can't." My smile faltered. He brushed his fingers along the side of my face and explained, "I promised my older sister Marie that I would babysit for my nephew, Max, tonight."

You babysit?" I asked, stunned.

"Yup. I'm a bona fide babysitter."

"Wow. You don't look like any babysitter I ever had growing up." I chuckled, roaming my eyes over his handsome face and great body. "My babysitters always were the old granny type who smelled like Earl Grey tea and mothballs."

"I may not be your typical babysitter, but I like watching Max. He's a good kid. We have fun together. Plus it keeps me out of trouble." He winked.

I was falling for him, fast and hard. It was impossible not to. I'd never met anyone like James. He was handsome, fun, and incredibly sweet. Maybe my mom was right. Nowhere was the right place for us. I was speechless.

James added, "I'm free tomorrow. It's Sunday, so I don't even have football practice. We could get together and do something fun. What do you think?"

I hesitated for a second.

"What's the matter?" James frowned. "Are you worried

that I'll stand you up again? I won't, I promise. Cross my heart." He drew an imaginary cross over his heart with his hand. "My dad will never come between us again," he stated emphatically.

"I know. It's not that." I shook my head. "Tomorrow I was going to borrow my mom's car to go shopping. The moving truck hasn't arrived yet with my art supplies and I'm running low. I wanted to stock up. It's no big deal, though. I can always go another day."

Relief flooded James' face and he rushed to say, "No, that's perfect. I'll take you. I have some back-to-school shopping to do. It'll give me a good excuse to get it done."

"Are you sure?" I asked, giving him a chance to back out.

"I'm positive. It'll be fun showing you around. We can make a day out of it." He beamed. Growing slightly more serious, he said, "This is a small city. I'm not sure you'll find what you're looking for." I couldn't help but smile. I'd already found what I was looking for. It was standing right in front of me. James took my smile as confirmation. "I'll pick you up at eleven, or is that too early for you?"

"Very funny." I playfully slapped him on the arm. "I'll be dressed and waiting for you."

"Okay, it's a date then."

"It's a date," I repeated.

He bent down and kissed me. The kiss was light and quick.

Pulling away, he said, "I have to go. I'll see you tomorrow."

I stood on the front porch and watched him drive away. I felt like a part of me left with him. I sighed.

Suddenly I remembered I had a phone call to make. I finally had the details Paige had asked for over a week ago. I ran into the house to find my phone.

Pops was sitting in his chair. "Have a good time, did you?" he called out.

I stopped and put my hands on my hips. "Yeah, thanks for setting me up," I said sternly. I couldn't stay mad, I was too happy. "I had no idea you were such a smooth operator. I always thought matchmakers were little old ladies, not grumpy old men," I teased.

He chuckled.

Chapter Twelve

Dooner

Mikayla was waiting for me on the porch swing. She looked beautiful. She wore a blue sundress and her hair was pulled back into a low ponytail. She stood as I made my way toward her. I was anxious to hold her in my arms again. Her skin was so soft and she smelled so sweet. I took a deep breath to calm myself. I gave her my word that we'd take things slow.

"Hi, James," she said, calling me by my given name. I liked how it sounded coming from her. It was like a fresh start. I wasn't Dooner, the football player, or Jimmy, the overworked farm boy. I was James—a good listener, a trusted friend, and hopefully something more.

"Come in for a sec. I want to tell my mom that you're here."

She held the front door open. I followed her inside. "Mom, you remember James, right? He gave me a ride home from school last week."

"How could I forget? Come on in, James. It's nice to see you again." Mrs. Mooney lightly placed her hand on my back, guiding me into the kitchen.

"Thanks. It's nice to see you again too."

Mr. Jenkins and Emma were sitting across from each other at the kitchen table. "Hello there, son," Mr. Jenkins said, shaking my hand.

"Hi, Dooner," Emma said. "Did you hear that I made the cheerleading squad? I'll be cheering you on from the sidelines during all the games this season. Maybe I can even be your cheerleader, if you're not already spoken for." She gushed, oblivious to the fact that I was holding her sister's hand. Mike tightened her grip.

"Ouch!" Emma snarled before I could decide how to respond without being rude. I couldn't be sure, but I thought I saw movement under the table. Mr. Jenkins winked at me as he continued to eat his toast.

Paying no attention to them, Mrs. Mooney spoke to us instead. "You two kids are going shopping?"

"Yes, Mom," Mikayla answered.

"I thought we'd get a bite to eat too, if that's okay," I added.

Mike smiled. "I'd like that."

"I won't wait dinner for you then. We'll see you whenever you get back. Do me a favor, though, and give me a call if you think you're going to be real late."

"No problem. We'll see you later." Mikayla waved to everyone as we exited.

Once we were settled into Old Faithful, I reached over and grabbed her hand again. When she was this close to me, I had to be touching her. We held hands and talked the whole ride into the city. Railroad Mills was a half an hour from everything—the tractor supply store, the movie theater, the airport, and shopping.

"I looked up a couple of specialized art stores on the internet, along with the larger arts and crafts chain stores. Which would you rather go to? I printed directions for each, so take your pick." I handed her the printouts.

"So you did homework?" I loved how her smile made her

eyes sparkle.

"You sound surprised. Didn't I tell you that I'm an A student? I always do my homework."

"Hold still, I think you have something on your nose." She brushed the tip of my nose with her finger. "I got it." She laughed.

"Very funny." I chuckled. I'd noticed that I'd been laughing more the last couple of days. Until I met Mikayla, I didn't really have many reasons to laugh. I enjoyed her sense of humor. She brought out the best in me.

Mike studied the papers and then said, "I'd love to check out one of the smaller stores. Here's one with a promising name. 'The Artist's Studio.' Its address is 1235 Park Avenue, let's go there."

"Sounds good to me." I liked a girl who was decisive.

A little while later, we pushed open the door to the art store. I could tell that Mikayla felt at home among the endless supplies. A smile never left her face. She browsed the store looking at paints, canvases, pencils, and things that I couldn't even identify. I wasn't the artistic type. I could only draw stick figures. Eventually she bought several drawing pads, pencils, and a sharpener.

Skipping on the way out, she exclaimed, "Thanks for bringing me. It reminds me of an art store that I loved to shop at in San Francisco. I didn't really expect to find one here of the same quality. They even carry my favorite brand of shading pencils." She proudly held up her shopping bag.

"It sounds like you have another reason to like it here," I pointed out.

"You're right. I do." She grinned.

We reached Old Faithful. Before opening the truck door for her, I said, "I could remind you of the other reason." My lips hovered an inch away from hers, causing her breath to come in shallow gasps.

"I think you should," she whispered just loud enough for

me to hear.

I touched my lips to hers. Heat instantly coursed through my body. I'd never experienced such bliss from a simple kiss. I wanted more. I pushed my tongue into her mouth and tasted her. She was like pure honey. I pulled her even closer. I liked feeling her heart beat next to mine. She ran her hands through my hair and I sighed. It was hard not to get carried away, but I had given her my word. I pulled away, and pressed my forehead against hers. "You take my breath away."

"I know the feeling," she panted.

Needing a distraction, I reached around her and opened the truck door. "Let's eat. I'm starving."

"You're always hungry," she teased. "Where do you put it all?" She shook her head, looking bewildered. She climbed into the cab.

"I don't know." I shrugged, closing the door. "Do you like barbeque?"

"Yeah."

"Good. Have you ever been to the Dinosaur Barbeque?"

"No. We hardly ever came into the city during our visits. We always spent all of our time at the farm."

"You're going to love the food at this joint." As if to prove it, my stomach rumbled.

The place was jamming for a Sunday afternoon. We waited to sit down, hanging out on the outdoor patio, watching the motorcycles come and go. Finally we were called and the hostess led us to a table inside. The smell of barbecue made my mouth water.

"What do you usually order?" Mikayla asked me while poring over the menu.

"I have lots of favorites. Sometimes I get the pulled pork sandwich, the beef brisket, or the ribs."

"I love ribs. Do you want to get the sweetheart deal for two? It says it comes with a full rack of ribs and four sides to share. You can pick two sides that you like and I can pick two that I like."

"Sounds great." I didn't tell her that usually I ate the full rack and four sides all by myself. I didn't want to seem like a pig.

We placed our order and then I grabbed her hand. I couldn't believe my strong desire to be close to her. I'd never felt like this before. I couldn't seem to get enough of her. "I've never met anyone like you," I confessed, staring into her deep brown eyes.

She raised one eyebrow. "What exactly does that mean?"

"It's a good thing. You're different than all the other girls I've ever met. You're honest, you aren't afraid to speak your mind, and you're fun to be with." She relaxed. I wanted to tell her that I was falling for her, and hard, but I didn't want to scare her. "I like hanging with you."

She blushed—she looked adorable when she blushed. "I like hanging out with you too."

"Do you want to play twenty questions again, while we wait for our food? I've been thinking of questions I want to ask you."

"Sure, but I go first," she said with a devilish grin.

"You went first yesterday." I sounded like a little kid on the playground.

"I know." She shrugged.

She was so beautiful, and I wanted her so badly, that I knew I'd have a hard time denying her anything she wanted. "Okay. Shoot."

"How many girlfriends have you had?" she asked, surprising me. Now I understood the grin.

"Why do you want to know?"

"Just curious? You said I wasn't like any girl you'd ever met, so it got me wondering how many girlfriends you've had."

"I've never had a girlfriend," I stated, which was the truth. I'd hooked up with a couple of girls, but I'd never had a girlfriend.

"No way," she exclaimed. "You expect me to believe that you've never had a girlfriend?"

"It's true. I've never had a girlfriend," I repeated, hoping she'd see I was telling the truth. "Why's that so hard to believe?"

"You're totally hot, for one thing." It was my turn to blush. I knew girls thought I was handsome, but to hear Mikayla say it point-blank made me feel uncomfortable. She continued, "You're the star football player in a town where people eat, sleep, and breathe football." My cheeks got even hotter. "You're smart." I was speechless. "And fun to be with. I thought for sure you'd had lots."

"I guess I could've had a girlfriend if I'd wanted one. I'd never met anyone who I liked, until now." I was still holding her hand and I squeezed it. "What about you? I bet you've had lots of boyfriends."

"No. I've never had a boyfriend. Like you, I never met anyone I cared enough about, until now."

Suddenly I was the happiest I'd ever been in my life. I couldn't believe I met someone as special as Mikayla, and like me, she'd never been in a serious relationship. Things were beginning to sound too good to be true. I never had anything I ever really wanted before, and I kept waiting for something to go wrong. Pushing all negative thoughts out of my head, I seized the moment and kissed her full lips. We were here together now and that was all that mattered.

"My turn. What's on your playlist?" I asked, pulling away and totally changing the subject.

"I have songs by Cold Play, the Fray, Katie Perry, Adele. I don't have any country, that's for sure."

"You'll come around. You'll see." I loved country music and if I had any say in it, Mikayla soon would too. She'd look hot as hell wearing a pair of her short jean shorts with cowboy boots and a hat.

"I doubt it," she declared, shaking her head. I enjoyed a

good challenge and couldn't wait to prove her wrong.

"What's your favorite subject at school?" she asked. "I already know you do your homework."

I smiled at her light teasing. "Math. What about you?"

"Art."

Just then the waitress arrived with our food. We made quick work out of the ribs and the accompanying sides.

"You were right. That was the best barbeque I've ever had. Thanks for bringing me here." She leaned back and patted her stomach. "I'm stuffed. I think I ate as much as you."

I laughed. "I'm glad you enjoyed it."

I threw enough money down on the table to cover the bill and we left.

"Thanks," she said as we walked back to my truck.

"My pleasure."

"Where to next?" It made me happy that she wasn't ready for our date to end.

"The mall? I need to buy a new pair of jeans."

"Sounds good to me."

I wasn't much of a shopper. We weren't at the mall for more than five minutes when I grabbed two pairs of jeans and got in line to pay.

"You're not going to try them on?" She sounded surprised..

"Nope, I already know these fit. I buy the same ones every time. Guys are all business when it comes to shopping. We get in and we get out. However, when it comes to important things, I take my time." I winked.

She playfully bumped me in the arm. "Good to know."

Searching for something else to do, I suggested, "Hey, let's go check out a new game place that opened up earlier this summer. It's in a plaza across the street. I haven't been there yet."

"Let's go."

A few minutes later I held open the door to the arcade.

marysue g. hobika

This place had it all—video games, simulators, carnival games, pool and air hockey tables, and even a five-lane bowling alley. I bought a card with unlimited games for two hours. She tried to pay, but there was no way I was allowing it. I asked her out and I wanted to do things right, and that included paying.

"So what's your favorite game?" I asked.

"Skee-ball," she answered without hesitation. "My dad took Emma and me to the Pier Saturday afternoons when we were kids. He gave us each our own money to spend. I always went straight to the Skee-ball machines. I saved all of my tickets, week after week, until I had enough to turn them in for a giant stuffed animal. I picked a huge, brown teddy bear that was twice as big as I was." She laughed. I could easily picture her standing there, the giant bear almost knocking her over, but too proud to let anyone else carry it for her. "Emma turned in her tickets each week. She always ended up with the same carnival garbage. I'd rather be patient and walk away with the grand prize in the end." She grinned and then looped her arm through mine.

"We have something in common then." Mikayla was my grand prize. "There are things worth waiting for." We wandered around, looking for the Skee-ball machines.

"What about you? What's your favorite game?"

"I don't have a favorite game." Her face fell. Not wanting to disappoint her, I quickly said, "I do, however, have a favorite carnival ride." I took a deep breath. I rarely talked about myself, and least of all my childhood, but this felt right. "One summer when I was seven, my dad took me to the carnival when it came to town. I'd never been before and I was thrilled to finally go. I couldn't believe my luck when he handed me a five-dollar bill and told me that I could spend it on whatever I wanted. Then he disappeared into the beer tent, saying he'd find me later. I immediately ran over to the ticket booth and used all the money to buy tickcts for the rides before he could come back and change his mind. The scrambler was my favorite ride. I loved the speed and the way it tossed me around inside of the cart. I rode it again and again. By the time I ran out of tickets, it was getting dark and my dad still hadn't come to get me. I was sure he'd gotten drunk and forgotten. I was hungry and ready to go home, so I started walking, when suddenly my mom pulled up in a borrowed truck."

"You must have been scared," Mike declared.

"No, I wasn't scared," I answered truthfully, shaking my head. I'd been relieved. My father had forgotten me, so I actually got to enjoy myself. He was a mean drunk. I didn't tell her that though because I worried it would change how she felt about me if she knew.

"I would've been scared," she stated.

"I doubt that." I smirked, thinking back to the night I met her. "Aren't you the girl who wanted to walk home alone in the dark on unfamiliar country roads?"

She laughed and her cheeks turned pink. "Yeah, but some rogue cowboy wouldn't hear of it."

"He must be one of the good guys," I teased.

Suddenly she shouted excitedly, "I see the Skee-ball machines. Right over there." She pointed to the back right hand corner. "Let's go play." Her enthusiasm was contagious. For the first time in my life, I was looking forward to playing Skee-ball.

The two hours flew by. We played everything from Skee-ball to video games. We raced each other on motorcycles and on ski-dos. It was an afternoon I wouldn't soon forget. We left carrying an oversized horse between the two of us.

I carefully placed it in the back of my pick-up and tied it down with some old rope while Mikayla jumped in the cab. When I got in, I smiled to find her sitting in the middle, right next to me.

"I can't believe you won that huge horse for me. It took me months of saving tickets to get one. Thanks." She leaned over and kissed me on the cheek.

"My pleasure." She was positively beaming. I loved how easy it was to make her smile. I only hoped I could continue to make her happy. Because making her happy felt so good. Not even football made me feel like this.

We continued to get to know each other on the way home, covering all sorts of topics. We talked about school, classes, teachers, and friends. We joked and laughed. We flirted. Her sweet lavender sent filled the small confines of the cab. Her gorgeous body pressed against mine, testing my limits. Several times I almost pulled over to the side of the road to make love to her, but of course I didn't. I kept my promise to be patient. She was completely unaware of the effect she had on me.

We arrived back at the farm and I quickly jumped out. I needed the fresh air to calm my raging hormones. I ran around to the back of the truck and untied the horse. "When can I see you again?" I asked, setting it down on the front porch.

"Tomorrow?" she said hopefully. "I'll be here all day, hanging out with Pops." She tucked a curl behind her ear. "You're the one with the busy schedule."

"Shit," I said, frowning. I forgot all about two-a-days. Hell, who was I kidding? I forgot everything when I was with Mikayla. When I was with her, it was like nothing else existed. "How about after dinner? I can stop over then."

"That sounds great. I'll be here." She smiled brightly. Her smile was intoxicating. I've never been drunk, but it must be similar to what I was experiencing right now.

"I'll come by around seven." I leaned down and gave her a light peck on the cheek. I didn't trust myself to give her anything more. My blood was still boiling. I opened the front door for her and all but pushed her and the stuffed horse inside.

It had been hours since lunch and I was starving. I hurried home, hoping to find a pot of soup on the stove or a roast in the oven. When I walked into the kitchen, I knew instantly that something was wrong. My mom wasn't in the kitchen, like always. It was dinnertime, yet it didn't smell like it. There could only be one reason why.

I stormed into the living room. My dad was sitting in his battered chair, watching TV. Only I doubted he even knew what show was on. His eyes were too glazed over. He had a drink in his hand and a half empty bottle of whisky on the table next to him.

"What's going on?" I confronted him. "Where's Mom?"

"She's in her room," he said, slurring his words. I looked toward the stairs. He saw me and explained, "Leave her alone. She doesn't want to see you." My dad wasn't making sense. He got out of his chair to face me, swaying so much that he almost fell over. He was the drunkest I'd seen him in years. His breath was so bad that I felt drunk just from sharing the same air. "We heard that you've been benched for the opening game."

Shit. He wasn't supposed to find out. I figured Coach would change his mind by game time and my dad would never have been the wiser. I should have known better. People in this town love to gossip, especially about their football team and star players. My dad must have heard about it and taken it out on my mom because I wasn't here. My eyes hardened as I imagined the scene that took place. My fists clenched at my sides. I felt sick with guilt. "Why'd you have to take it out on Mom? Your beef is clearly with me." I pointed a finger at my chest.

"Your mom's fine. Like I said, she doesn't want to see you."

I knew he was lying. The sad truth was it didn't matter. She would defend his actions just like she'd been doing for as long as I could remember. Yet I couldn't stop myself from saying, "Next time, leave her out of it."

"Don't you tell me what to do." His anger piqued, he shouted, "What were you thinking, you dumb ass?" Seeing the ashtray, he picked it up and threw it at me. I ducked and watched as it hit the wall, spilling ashes and cigarette butts everywhere.

I knew my dad was trying to pick a fight with me, but it wasn't going to work. I refused to be like him. "What were *you* thinking?" I snarled through clenched teeth.

Ignoring me, he said, "You better get your act together and fast. There'll be hell to pay if you don't play in that game. You hear me, boy?"

"Don't worry, I got a plan." Under my breath I muttered, "I want that scholarship more than you know."

Chapter Thirteen

Mike

It was Friday evening. Pops was already sitting in his chair in the family room, working on another crossword puzzle while watching a baseball game on TV. I thought about joining him until James got here, but I couldn't stand the heat in the house. I could barely breathe, it was so hot. I didn't understand how he survived without central air. I raised my hand in a friendly wave before walking out onto the porch. I sighed in relief. Thankfully it was several degrees cooler out here.

I sat down on the porch swing, marveling at how quickly evenings had become my favorite part of the day. The locusts buzzed in the trees. Occasionally loud trucks rumbled by. I gently rocked back and forth. These country sounds were almost as comforting to me as the city sounds had been.

Not two feet away, I watched a robin fly in and out of a nearby shrub. The mama bird kept returning with a delicious treat for her hungry babies, who couldn't fly yet. Protecting them, providing for them, she put their needs even before her own. I couldn't help but think of my own mother. I was sure those were the very same reasons why she'd moved us here to

Nowhere. I couldn't deny that I'd been angry at her. Smiling, I realized I no longer felt that way.

James. He was the reason for my change of heart. I continued to smile. It was Fate, meeting him on my very first night here at a party I didn't even want to go to. As I thought back to that night I laughed out loud, causing the bird to fly away again. We'd come far since our initial encounter.

My heart quickened as I thought about how he'd be here soon. I couldn't wait to see his handsome face, deep dimples, and green eyes. I wanted to run into his strong arms and have him hold me tight. Heat spread across my body as I dreamed about the kiss we'd share.

Slam!

I jumped. *What the—*? I looked up and saw Emma. "Did you have to slam the door so hard?" I complained. I was just getting to the good part.

She shrugged.

"This is an old house, you know." Wow, I sounded just like Pops. I guess we did spend a lot of time together.

"What's your problem?" she hissed.

I narrowed my eyes as I zoned in on the fact that she was wearing my favorite jean skirt, without my permission. "Where do you think you're going wearing my skirt?" I snapped. I hated it when Emma borrowed my clothes. She rarely returned anything. When she did, it was only because it was ruined.

"I have a date tonight with Casey." She stuck her chin in the air. "We're going to the movies with Tyler and Liz."

"You're going out with Casey?" I asked in disbelief. "He's a jerk."

"You don't even know him," she said defensively.

"I know him, all right." I only talked to him the night of the party, but it had only taken a few seconds to realize he was full of himself. I didn't hold back. "Casey is a conceited asshole who only cares about one person. Himself. I'm also willing to bet he's only interested in one thing."

"You're wrong. You're just jealous because Casey asked me out and not you," she yelled.

I rolled my eyes. I could tell her about Casey hitting on me at the party and asking me if I wanted him to show me around, but I didn't. She wouldn't listen anyway. Instead, I gave her a warning. "Just be careful. Casey may not be the guy you think he is."

"Whatever." She shrugged. "What makes you think James is so wonderful?" She emphasized his name, mocking me.

"Lots of reasons," I stated matter-of-factly. I wasn't going to discuss what was happening between James and I with Emma.

"Really?" she laughed. "Haven't you heard? He sleeps around." I kept my face blank, giving nothing away. I knew Emma was just trying to get back at me for talking trash about her date, even though everything I said had been the truth. What came out of her mouth was nothing but lies. "He uses girls. He has sex with them, and then the next day he acts like he doesn't know them."

"Says who? One of your cheerleader friends who feeds off of gossip and spreads rumors to make herself feel better?" My voice rose.

"It was from a very reliable source."

"I'm sure. Too bad it doesn't make any sense." I knew Dooner, and he would never do that.

"Believe what you want. Just remember I did try to warn you." *What? I was the one trying to warn her.* She turned to leave; only I caught her by her arm.

"Take my skirt off," I demanded. I knew I was being childish, but I didn't care. Emma had gone too far, and now I was pissed.

"No way. I look good in this." She put her hands on her hips.

"Too bad. Take it off. I don't want you wearing my skirt

while that idiot you're going out with tries to get his hand under it."

"Be serious, Mike." I remained unwavering, glaring at her sternly. Emma shifted uneasily and tried a different tactic. "Please let me wear it. I don't have time to change," she pleaded.

No way was I backing down. "Last chance. Now take it off before I take it off for you." I heard the engine of Tyler's truck coming down the road. I nodded my head. "I'd hurry if I were you."

Emma huffed. She knew me well enough that if I said something I meant it. "You're such a bitch," she shouted, running inside to change before I could follow through with my threat and humiliate her.

Just as the door slammed, Tyler pulled in. It did look like it was a double date. Liz was sitting shotgun while Casey sat alone in the back. I slowly approached as Tyler rolled down his window.

"Hiya Mike. Where's Emma?" Tyler asked, leaning out the window.

"She's coming. She had a last minute wardrobe change." I smiled.

"Tell her to hurry, would ya. "

"I'm sure she'll be right out. You guys are going to the movies, huh?"

"Yeah. What are your plans? There's room for one more, if you want to go," Tyler offered. It was clear by the look on Liz's face that she hoped I didn't take him up on it. If James weren't coming over, then I'd tag along just to piss her off. I wasn't sure what I had ever done to her, I had only met her once, but it was obvious she didn't like me.

Casey rolled down his window and shouted enthusiastically, "Yeah, you should come. Then I'd have one beautiful sister on each arm. A hot threesome's one of my fantasies."

"Gross." *This guy's even worse than I thought.*

He laughed. "Can't blame a guy for trying. But it's probably for the best anyway. It doesn't look as if your sister's in the mood to share."

Emma came up behind me, scowling. "What's going on, Mike?"

"Nothing. Just letting them know you'd be out in a minute."

"Well, I'm here now," she said, all but pushing me out of the way to climb into the back next to Casey. She'd changed into a whole new outfit. She had on the shortest pair of shorts she owned and a super tight v-neck T-shirt that flaunted her chest. I rolled my eyes. I didn't understand why Emma thought Casey needed encouragement.

"Sure you don't want to come?" asked Tyler one last time, chuckling.

"No thanks." I waved as they pulled away.

I was too restless to sit on the swing. I paced back and forth on the driveway, replaying the fight with Emma. I didn't believe a word she said about James. She was just jealous because he picked me over her. I bet her new cheerleading friends had filled her ears with untrue rumors. I hated to stereotype, but wasn't that what cheerleaders did? I knew James had a past. Didn't everybody? What mattered was that we were together now.

By the time James arrived, I'd carved a noticeable path in the stone driveway. "Is everything okay?" He sounded concerned.

"I had a big fight with Emma."

"Do you want to talk about it?"

"No, not really. It'll blow over in a couple of days." I shrugged, not letting Emma's comments cause friction between me and James. I trusted him and what we had together.

"Okay. Is there anything I can do?" He grabbed my hand

and squeezed it.

"No." Smirking, I added, "A kiss would make me feel better." I reached up and wrapped my arms around his neck. He leaned down and softly kissed me. Instantly, I relaxed. The kiss deepened and quickly became urgent. Our tongues intertwined. The rest of the world ceased to exist. Eventually we pulled apart to catch our breaths.

While standing in the middle of the driveway, waiting for our breathing to return to normal, he asked, "What do you want to do tonight?"

There really wasn't anything in a town this small for teens to do, and partying on a dirt road once was more than enough for me. Happily I suggested, "I'm hot. Let's go for a swim."

James' bright green eyes twinkled. He liked my idea. "I thought you'd never ask."

This time we didn't wade in the creek. Anxious to cool off, we headed directly to the pond. "Last one in is a rotten egg!" I challenged playfully.

"You're on." he declared.

Without pause we stripped down to our undergarments, racing to be the first one to jump in.

I laughed as James fell over trying to pull off one of his cowboy boots. "Mike, help me. I need a hand," he pleaded.

"Why? So you can pull me down too? I'm not falling for that trick," I smirked, leaving him on the ground. I quickly spun around and jumped in. The cold water felt refreshing against my hot skin. I came up laughing just as James jumped in, joining me.

James and I swam around for at least an hour, showing off for each other. We even attempted to reenact the lift scene from the movie "Dirty Dancing," laughing and sputtering water the whole time. "That wasn't how they did it in the movie." I laughed after our fourth failed attempt.

"Are you saying I shouldn't give up my football dream to become a dancer," he teased, feigning hurt.

"Definitely not." I splashed him full in the face.

I closed my mouth, preparing to be splashed back. Only he surprised me by catching me in his arms. "Now, if you promise not to splash again, I'll let you go." He laughed.

"What if I don't want you to let me go?" I said, seriously. His smile lit up his whole face.

"Then I won't." He pulled me even closer and kissed me. I trembled in his arms. Pulling away, he said, "You're freezing. Let's get out." I wasn't trembling because I was cold, but I didn't correct him. I followed him out onto the rocks where he wrapped his strong arms around me.

Looking into his loving face, I made up my mind. I chose James and I chose now. I kissed him passionately while running my hands across his bare back, like I'd daydreamed about earlier. My mouth left his as I began to kiss his neck, then his shoulder, making a trail down his chest. I moved off of the rock to kneel on the ground to continue tasting him, when he stopped me.

"What are you doing?" he asked, breathing heavily.

"I'm getting to know you better," I answered shyly. "Why, did I do something wrong?" I fretted.

He ran his hand through his sandy colored hair. "No." He took a shaky breath. "I can't believe I'm going to say this, but the problem is that I can't let you do what you were about to do." *I'm confused.* He took another deep breath. Steadier this time. "I promised you, we would take things slow." *Now I understand.* He tucked a wet curl behind my ear.

"It's okay. I want to." I boldly put his hand on my breast. He inhaled and quickly pulled his hand away.

I was wrong. He hasn't been waiting for me to give him permission. Blinking back tears, I whispered, "I get it. You're not interested in me like that." I made a move to break free of his embrace. Only he tightened his hold.

Exasperated, he said, "You're crazy, you know that?" He sighed and then gently continued. "What I'm trying to say is that while I'm dying to know what it feels like to make love to you, this is not the time or the place." He held my face in his hand, so that I had to look at him. He was telling the truth. "You're upset right now because you had a fight with Emma. I want you when you want me for all the right reasons." He rubbed his thumb along my jaw and then dropped his hand.

"You think the only reason I want to be with you is so that I can forget about a fight I had with my sister?"

"Look, Mikayla, I'm not very good with words. I care about you." He looked up at the night sky and then back at me. "Who am I kiddin'? I've fallen in love with you." He paused, letting that sink in. "I keep thinking about what you said about wanting more this time. About waiting until you're in love before you have sex again. I'm in love with you, but are you ready to say the same about me?" I blushed. I knew I had real feelings for James, but I hadn't put a label on them yet. Recognizing my silence as confirmation that I wasn't ready, he continued. "It's okay. We have lots of time." He pulled me against his chest and kissed the top of my head.

We sat in silence for several minutes. The creek bubbled in the background. "Okay, not tonight, but soon," I said into his bare chest. Looking into his understanding deep green eyes, I confessed, "I'm scared. The truth is I've never felt like this before. When we're together my heart races and I'm afraid it's going to explode right out of my chest. Even the slightest brush of your fingers makes my skin feel like it's on fire."

"I know how you feel."

Our lips met somewhere in the middle, as if we were sealing an invisible agreement to wait until we were both ready. We kissed carefully, holding ourselves back from getting carried away.

"It's getting dark. We better get back, you didn't even tell your mom we were going on a walk," James said, pulling away.

We quickly dressed. It was a quiet walk back, but not an uncomfortable one. We were each lost in our own thoughts. By the time we exited the cornfield, the sun had set and the stars were out.

Breaking the silence, I exclaimed, "Wow, I'm still amazed by how beautiful the night sky is here in Nowhere. I love looking up at the stars. I missed out on skies like this living in San Francisco. There was too much smog and too many lights."

"Really? I couldn't imagine being happy in a place where I couldn't see the stars. When I can't sleep, which is often, I look out my bedroom window to study them. It helps me relax. They remind me that I'm only a tiny part of the universe."

He was quickly becoming my whole universe, but I wasn't ready to tell him that yet. Instead a shared a different piece of my heart, "The stars remind me of my dad. When I was four years old he put glow-in-the-dark star stickers on the ceiling above my bed. At the time I was having terrible nightmares and he said that the stars would protect me. I believed him and the nightmares disappeared completely. When my dad died, the nightmares returned. They're even worse than when I was a kid." I shivered. "I wished I still believed star stickers would keep them away."

"Here you have the real stars." Squeezing my hand, he added, "And me."

I sighed. *Could James be any more perfect?* I knew with certainty that Emma had been wrong about him. Any remaining doubts I had, vanished. Speaking truthfully I said, "I do feel safe when I'm with you. I just wish you didn't have to leave. If only there was a way you could stay so that I could sleep peacefully like I did that day by the pond." We were back to where we started, standing in the driveway, facing each other.

"Hmmm," James said thoughtfully. *Was he trying to think of a way to sneak into my room in the middle of the night?* I wondered. I'd love to have him hold me all night long, but I knew it wasn't possible. He was only human after all, unlike Edward or Jacob from the "Twilight" series; they easily jumped up two stories to visit Bella in her bedroom at night.

"So what's your plan?" I asked impatiently, waiting for James to explain what he was thinking.

"It's nothing." I raised my eyebrows, not believing him. The color of his eyes confirmed that he was hiding something, but I was confident it wasn't anything bad.

Shaking it off, he said, "I just wish I could stay, so you could sleep." He lightly brushed a curl away from my eyes.

Pulling me close, he kissed me like never before. He didn't hold back, and neither did I. My heart grew twice its size inside my chest. I knew without a doubt it belonged to James.

Moments later when he left, I stood rooted to the spot, calling out into the night what I hadn't been ready to say in the woods, "I love you, James."

Chapter Fourteen

Dooner

Sweat ran down my back, soaking my T-shirt. My hair was so wet it looked like I'd just stepped out of the shower. It was only nine o'clock in the morning, but already it was a scorcher. Tyler and I had been throwing passes and running drills for an hour, trying to prove that we meant business. The rest of the team would be here soon.

Our plan had been going well so far. We were perfecting our passing patterns, like the square-out, the hook, and the fly. Tyler's arm was getting stronger; he was throwing the ball further and with greater accuracy. I, of course, had been catching them all. Casey met us every morning to play safety. He was a good blocker, but I was fast. Also I had the uncanny ability to be able to anticipate where Tyler was going to throw the ball. I always managed to get there just as the ball came down, landing in my outstretched hands. It was as if we could read other's minds.

Since today was Saturday, Tyler and I were on our own, running through drills that didn't necessarily require a blocker. Tyler was working on his bullet throw, using his arm strength to fire the ball. He'd throw the ball and I'd run, cutting sharply across the field toward the sideline. Once the ball was safe in my hands I'd step out of bounds to stop the clock, completing the square-out pattern. This was an excellent strategy in order to complete a first down. We did this over and over again.

In the background, I thought I heard someone climb the bleachers, but I didn't let it break my concentration. Like the ten times before, I rolled my shoulder toward the inside and cut quickly to the sideline. Catching the ball, I stepped out of bounds. It was a perfect play. At the same time, Tyler and I looked up to see who was watching us. It was Coach. We could only hope this was a good sign. We finished up and went inside to meet the rest of the boys. Coach left without saying a word.

Jogging in, I commented, "I think we can cross 'square-out' off our list of passing patterns. We nailed it."

"Yeah, man. I was in the zone just now." Growing more serious, he said, "I just wish Coach would hurry up and put us back in the starting line-up. He must've seen how well we connected today."

"Yeah, I'm sure he did. I think he's going to make us sweat it out a little longer. He's going to make us work hard for a second chance. We just have to keep doing what we've been doing. He'll come around. It may not be until the last minute before the game begins, but he will." I put my complete faith in Coach recognizing the value we brought to the team. What other choice did I have?

"I hope you're right," Tyler stated.

Me too.

Coach was sitting in his office, staring at his playbook, when we passed by on our way into the locker room. He glanced in our direction, giving us the briefest of smiles. It wasn't much encouragement, but it was a start.

I pushed open the locker room door, while Tyler walked on. He headed toward the gym with a different agenda in mind. I was willing to bet he was meeting Liz in the 'secret make-out corner'—a small area that was blocked by the bleachers—although that was a misnomer because students did a lot more than just make out. She was probably running her red fingernails down his chest right now, I chuckled to myself thinking they deserved each other.

It was loud in the locker room as the guys joked around while getting on their gear. Unfortunately, most of them were still pissed about the suicides, but they were beginning to come around. Like Coach, they could see that Tyler and I worked out our differences. Also they knew they needed us to have another undefeated season.

"Heya, Dooner," Ray said, grabbing his helmet.

"Hey," I responded, quickly grabbing my helmet too. "Alright if I walk with you?" I asked. I didn't think Ray would mind; he wasn't one to hold a grudge.

"Sure." He nodded.

Doing my part to make amends, I said, "You made a great play yesterday. You closed the gap on the runner in record time. What's your time for the 40?"

"I run the 40 in 6.21 seconds," he said modestly.

"Wow, man, that's great. We should come up with a defensive strategy to capitalize on your speed and strength." I wanted the team to know they mattered.

"Cool." Ray grinned proudly.

During the entire practice I could feel Coach's eyes on me—watching, waiting. I made sure I didn't screw up. I caught every pass that Tyler threw me. I encouraged the guys and helped them work on their game. By the time practice ended, I was feeling optimistic.

I hurried home and was whistling a Tim McGraw song when the kitchen door closed behind me. My mom was standing at the sink, drying dishes while my dad sat eating a huge slice of rhubarb pie. The house was quiet. For once, my dad wasn't yelling or cursing.

"Hey," I said, acknowledging them both.

"Hi, Sweetie," my mom said, placing a plate in the cupboard.

My dad simply grunted. We hadn't said more than two words to each other since the big blowup. I had nothing to say to him.

Turning quickly, I grabbed a cold Gatorade out of the refrigerator. I took a long sip as I continued to stare inside, avoiding eye contact. I'd been trying to keep a low profile. "What's for lunch? I'm starving."

"I made you a couple of tuna fish sandwiches," my mom answered, smiling. "They're in the container with the blue lid on the top shelf."

"Thanks, mom." I pulled it out and joined my dad at the table.

I wasn't going to be the one to break the ice. I didn't mind eating my lunch in silence; I preferred it. I kept my eyes down on my plate, hoping to avoid another confrontation.

"How was practice today, honey?" my mom asked.

Great, here we go. "Good," I answered, saying as little as possible.

"What does that mean?" my dad asked speaking to me for the first time in days.

"It means that practice was good."

"Did Coach finally smarten up and put you back in the game?"

I didn't like it when he spoke poorly of Coach. He was only doing what he thought was right. "No."

"Well, why the hell not?"

No matter what I said, it would be the wrong thing. Choosing my words carefully, I said, "He did see Tyler and me working on our passing game before practice today."

"What do you mean, your passing game?"

"We've been working every day before practice to perfect some new plays this season. We want to throw the ball, not just run it like all the other high school teams around here. Tyler has a strong arm and I'm able to catch anything. We want to show Coach that we can take the team to a whole new level." I didn't know why I told him all that, but I guess on some level I was still looking for my old man's approval.

"Tell me more," my dad said, leaning in closer. "Can you catch the ball even when you got a man blocking you?" I nodded. "I hope I won't see any interceptions or fumbles this year."

"I'm not going to fumble the ball," I said with anger. I was a better player than that. I hadn't fumbled once since playing varsity.

"That's my boy. Keep it up and Coach will have no choice but to play you." This was the most praise I'd receive from my dad. He wasn't one to hand out compliments.

"That's the plan," I confirmed.

""Now, Martha, get me another piece, would you? All this football talk has made me hungry. Give the boy a piece too, to keep his strength up."

My mom gladly placed a piece of pie in front of each of us. I knew it made her happy that my dad and I actually were talking again and even managed to have a civil conversation. The pie tasted great, practically melting in my mouth. "This is really good, Mom."

"Thanks." She smiled.

I quickly finished eating and placed the dirty plate in the sink. I had plans with Mikayla. With my stomach full, I was ready to leave. I grabbed my keys off the hook hanging by the back door. Looking over my shoulder I said, "Bye. I'll see you guys later. Thanks for the lunch, Mom. And the pie." I was anxious to leave while everyone was in a good mood.

"Hey, where you off to, son? More football practice? Do you and your buddies have plans to watch the videos from last year of the other teams?" my dad questioned, hopefully.

"No," I replied. It wasn't the answer he was looking for, so

I didn't tell him where I was headed. I was trying to avoid him getting pissed off again.

I felt his eyes studying me. "Ah, I see." A look dawned across his face. "It's a girl. Well, you better watch out," he warned, his face turning dark.

"Watch out for what?"

"Really? Are you that stupid, boy? Girls are nothing but trouble. The last thing you need right now is some tease throwing herself at you and then tricking you by getting pregnant. If that happens, you can kiss your scholarship goodbye."

My mom dropped the plate she was drying. It shattered on the old hardwood floor. "That's not how it happened."

It wasn't a secret that my parents got married because my mom was pregnant with my older sister. Although I doubted she tricked him. He wasn't the only one who had to change his plans regarding the future. He never remembered that part. He only ever thought about the fact that he was forced to give up a scholarship to play football, which he'd regretted ever since. But that was his story, not mine. I'd never do anything to hurt Mikayla, like get her pregnant. We hadn't even had sex yet. If and when we did, I'd be smart enough to wear a condom.

"Jesus, Martha, be more careful. Do you think that dishes grow on trees?" my dad shouted, snapping me out of my thoughts.

"It was an accident," she said, her voice cracking.

I grabbed the broom from the closet to sweep up the small pieces while she picked up the big ones. It seemed like I was always cleaning up one mess or another around here. I couldn't wait to move on.

I had my hand on the back door handle, when suddenly my dad was in my face. "Jimmy, remember—football is all that matters." I nodded, hoping to placate him. I was anxious to leave. "I better not hear that you're fooling around with some slut, or you'll be sorry. Keep your dick in your pants. You got that?"

"Yeah, Dad. I hear you loud and clear." I wiped his spit off my face with the back of my hand. Usually it was easiest to agree with him.

"Good." He stepped out of the way, allowing me to leave.

Chapter Fifteen

Mike

"Paige, hi," I said into my phone. "It's me, Mike." I was sitting on the porch, killing time before James arrived.

"Mike, is that really you? I barely recognize your voice anymore. You haven't called me all week."

"Sorry."

"You should be. I was beginning to worry that something happened to you. I thought maybe you fell into an old boarded-up water well, like Carrie did on 'Little House on the Prairie.' Do you remember that episode?"

"Yes, of course." My mom made us sit through re-runs of the show one summer just because they were her favorite books growing up.

"Is there one of those on your grandfather's property? If there is, then please stay away from it."

"Don't worry. There isn't one." I laughed. It was so like my best friend to be pessimistic. I missed her. "I've been busy, that's all."

"Huh? Busy doing what? You said yourself there's nothing to do in Nowhere." She sounded genuinely bewildered. I had complained to her many times how boring this place was.

"Trust me, Pops finds plenty for me to do. I swear we're the only two who do any work around here." I looked toward the vegetable stand and grinned proudly. "My mom's always at school and Emma's always hanging with her new cheerleading friends," I grumbled. I didn't want anyone to know that I enjoyed working around the farm with Pops. For an old guy, he was pretty cool. He was irritable, ornery, and sarcastic. We got along great.

"Like what? Plowing fields?" Paige wanted to know.

"No." I chuckled. "Pops doesn't farm crops anymore. He rents out the fields to another farmer. He's retired, except for the vegetable stand he operates, based on the honor system, at the side of the road. He sells surplus vegetables from his garden, and plants and flowers from the greenhouse. As a matter of fact, I just painted a new sign for it," I bragged, forgetting that I didn't want anyone to know that I liked it here.

"Holy crap. Who are you? And what have you done with my best friend? The day she's excited about a vegetable stand sign she painted, I know something's wrong."

I laughed heartily. "It does sound ridiculous, doesn't it?"

We laughed for a good five minutes. Abruptly Paige stopped and said, "Oh my God, it's the boy, isn't it? You're in love."

There was no use trying to deny it. We'd been friends for too long. Plus I was dying to talk about it. I'd told her all about the hike we went on, and other bits and pieces about James, but I hadn't told her how much he was beginning to mean to me. "Yeah, I am. He's amazing. It's all happening so fast, but it feels right."

"I can hear it in your voice. You sound happy."

"I am happy," I declared. "I'm beginning to think moving here wasn't such a bad idea after all."

"Wow."

"I know, right? Wait until you meet him next week. Then

you'll understand."

"I can't wait."

"Me either," I said, getting excited about Paige coming to visit for my eighteenth birthday. We'd been planning this since the day I left California. It had seemed such a long time to wait. I was surprised by how quickly time had passed.

"Tell me more about your cowboy?"

"Can't. He just pulled in. I gotta go," I said in a rush, watching as James hopped out of his truck wearing a button-down shirt, ripped jeans, and cowboy boots. I sighed.

"You go, girl. I'll call you when I get to the airport on Wednesday."

"Okay." I closed my phone as James bounded up the porch steps, two at a time. He sat down next to me, not even saying hello before kissing me fiercely on the lips.

"It's nice to see you too." I laughed.

"Was it too much?" He blushed.

"Never." I gently touched his face. James was so handsome—I still wasn't used to it.

His sandy brown hair was tousled, like he hadn't bothered to comb it when he got out of the shower. His face had two days worth of stubble, making him look rugged, in a good way.

Jumping up. I said, "I just had an idea. Wait here. Don't move." I rushed inside, returning a few minutes later with one of my new sketchpads and several freshly sharpened pencils. I didn't sit back down next to James; instead I pulled a chair over and sat down across from him.

"Is it okay if I sketch you?" I asked, flipping to a clean page.

"Sure," he answered. "Am I supposed to do anything special?"

"No, not really. Just relax."

"That sounds easy enough." He settled into the swing, resting one arm along the back of it. He stretched out his long legs in from of him. "How is this, relaxed enough?" I nodded.

"I feel strange sitting here without you next to me." He smiled.

"I know what you mean," I said, blushing. "You're doing great. Just stay still and be yourself."

I took my time. It wasn't easy to capture how truly handsome he was with mere paper and pencil. Maybe next time I'd try clay. I concentrated on his eyes and his facial expression. Those said a lot about a person. I'd noticed that his eyes changed color based on his mood. Right now they were a true clear green, which meant he was happy. When his eyes turned cloudy with a mix of grey, he was angry. But my favorite shade was clear dark green, the color of his eyes when he'd just kissed me. Eyes only told part of the story. Drawing a portrait could be like looking into a person's soul, when done right. I paid close attention to every detail. I was surprised to see that I'd only partially knocked down the wall that James built to protect himself. It was hard imagining a big tough guy like James needing a wall to feel safe. I wondered who'd hurt him. Was it an old girlfriend? I quickly rejected that idea because he claimed he'd never gotten emotionally attached to any girl until he met me. I thought I knew the real source. His father. He always got tense whenever his name was brought up. I couldn't explain it, but something didn't feel right.

The only noises were my pencil scratching and the occasional bird chirping. It was a comfortable silence. I wasn't sure how much time passed; I had a tendency to lose track when I was drawing. One hour could feel like five minutes.

"Can I look at the drawing when you're done?" James asked.

"Sure, I'll show you," I answered tentatively. This was the only area in my life where I lacked confidence. I felt vulnerable and exposed. Every piece of artwork I created was personal. It was a part of me. *What if James didn't like it?*

"What's the matter?"

"Nothing. It's just that...if you don't like it...Well, I don't take criticism well," I sputtered.

"Are you serious?" I nodded affirmatively.

"I'm going to love it," he exclaimed.

I still had my doubts, but I tried to sound positive, "Okay. I'm almost finished. Give me one more minute and then I'll show you. " I made several final strokes on the paper. Holding my breath, I handed him the sketchpad. I couldn't watch his reaction, in case it was bad, so instead I kept myself busy cleaning up my supplies.

He remained quiet, taking it all in, while my stomach was in knots. *Why isn't he saying anything? He must not like it.*

After several long minutes, he said, looking me in the eye, "I must confess, I don't know a lot about art, but this is really good. I mean *really* good. You're very talented." He handed the sketchpad back to me. I knew he meant what he said because his eyes were clear green. Also, he wouldn't have said that unless he meant it.

I smiled. "Thanks, I'm glad you like it." I said quietly. My face felt hot after hearing his compliment.

"Do you have any self-portraits?" he asked.

I thought for a minute. "No. At least not any recent ones." The last one I'd done was years ago.

"Would you draw one for me?" He used his foot to push the swing back and forth.

"You want me to draw a self-portrait and give it to you?" I repeated, making sure I hadn't misunderstood him.

"Well, yeah. You have one of me." He pointed at the sketchpad. "So it's only fair that I have one of you." He flashed me an irresistible smile.

Not only then would he have a drawing of mine, but it would be of me too. That felt very personal. Slowly I answered, "Okay, sure." His smile deepened. "I'll draw one tomorrow and give it to you when I see you."

"Perfect," he replied happily.

Suddenly I felt restless. We'd been sitting still for such a long time. Knowing James was probably hungry, I suggested,

"Come on, let's go see what's cooking in the kitchen,"

James laughed heartily. His laugh was full and robust. It had lost its rough edge. "Are you sure you haven't lived here your whole life? You're beginning to sound like a local."

I laughed too. "It's because I hang with Pops all the time. He's starting to rub off on me."

Once inside, we raided the fridge. Finding ground beef, I quickly turned it into burgers. James went out to the garden and picked a zucchini and yellow squash to add to the grill. There was nothing better than a cookout.

Pops was in the living room, watching baseball. I poked my head in. "Hey, Pops, James and I are making dinner. Are you in?" My mom and Emma weren't home.

"Absolutely. What are you making? Tomato sandwiches again?"

"No. We're cooking burgers on the grill."

"Even better."

"It should be ready in about ten minutes," I informed him.

"Okay. I'll be right out."

Soon the three of us were seated on the front porch with our plates on our laps.

"Great job grilling, son," said Pops. "These burgers are nice and juicy." As if to prove he was telling the truth, juice ran down his face when he took his next bite. He chuckled as he wiped it with a napkin.

"Thank you," James answered. I thought I saw his cheeks turn pink, but I couldn't be sure.

"I should have you guys cook for me all the time. I think I've gained about ten pounds since you all moved in." Pops patted his stomach.

"You look good, Pops." I smiled. It was true; he seemed younger than he did that first day.

We quickly finished everything on our plates. "That tasted awesome," I declared.

"It sure did. Thanks for asking me to join you young folk."

Pops' eyes were bright with appreciation.

"You're welcome," James and I said in unison, making us all laugh.

I stood to clean up, reaching for Pop-Pop's plate.

"No, you don't," he said, swatting my hand away. "I'm doing the dishes." James and I chuckled, because we were eating off of paper plates. Turning serious he added, "No, really. I got these." He stood and we handed him our plates. He disappeared into the house.

"I like your grandfather. He's a cool dude."

"Yeah, he is." I smiled. If we hadn't moved here, I wouldn't have had the chance to get to know Pops the way I knew him now. Once again, I was reminded that my mom had been right about moving to Nowhere.

"Here's some money," said Pops, coming back out onto the porch. He held a ten-dollar bill in his hand. "Go down to Blondie's and have a cone on me."

"Don't you want to come?" I asked.

"No, thanks. I'm full. The burger and vegetables hit the spot." He patted his stomach.

Slowly I took the money from his outstretched hand. "Thank you," I said, choking up a little.

"You're welcome. Now go." He practically shooed us off the porch. We were half way to James' truck, when he yelled, "Don't forget to bring me back the change." We laughed. Pops was back to sounding like himself.

Blondie's had the best homemade custard and waffle cones around. It was a local hot spot, open from Memorial Day to Labor Day. James had to wait until a family left before we could find an empty parking spot. "It looks the same," I commented, having been here many times on previous trips, I jumped down from his truck. James walked around and grabbed my hand. "I hope it tastes the same too."

"It does," James reassured me.

Now this was a scene I should draw, I thought to myself.

It was the epitome of summer in Nowhere. Families relaxing on benches while enjoying a cone together. Kids who had ice cream dripping down their arms because they couldn't lick them fast enough in the heat. Everyone talking and laughing. I tried to memorize it.

We walked up to the window. I ordered a medium twist; I could never decide which flavor I liked more, vanilla or chocolate. A twist was the best of both worlds. On the other hand, James knew exactly what he wanted. He ordered a large chocolate in a waffle cone.

Finding an empty picnic table, we sat across from each other.

"Hmm, you were wrong," I said, licking my cone.

"How's that?"

"It's better than I remember," I stated dreamily. James laughed.

"I'm glad you like it." He reached over to squeeze my hand.

"The west coast may have the market on great coffee, but the east coast has the best ice cream. And I'll take ice cream over coffee any day."

"You aren't kiddin'," agreed James, devouring his cone.

Looking at him, I noticed he had ice cream on his chin. "Hold still." I reached up and wiped it off with my finger. "Yum, chocolate is good." I licked my finger. "I still can't decide which flavor I like best."

"I know what I like best." James eyes had changed to a clear, dark green color. I leaned in closer. Just as our lips were about to touch, I felt someone standing over us. I looked up. It was Tyler, Liz, Emma, and Casey. *Great.*

"Hey Mike, Dooner," Tyler greeted us, frowning. "I didn't expect to see the two of you here. Together."

"We didn't expect to see you either," I retorted, giving Emma and Casey the same disapproving glare that Tyler was giving us.

James tried to be friendly and smooth things over. "We're just having a cone. Do you guys want to join us?" He moved his hand to indicate the rest of the table.

Before anyone could answer, Liz whined, "I don't know why we're here. I don't even eat ice cream."

I took a lick of my cone and said, "Really? You don't know what you're missing."

"I only eat fat-free Italian ice." She gave me a once over and then stuck her chin up in the air. If she was trying to imply that only fat girls ate ice cream, she was wrong. I ate ice cream all the time and I was anything but fat.

"That's too bad. Lucky for me, I don't have to worry about getting fat. I can eat the good stuff." I took another lick.

"Wow, you just got served," Casey snickered under his breath.

"Not cool, Mike," said Tyler looking even more pissed.

Without saying anything else, I walked over to the counter and grabbed a handful of napkins to prove how good I looked in my cut-off jeans. Normally I didn't like to show off, but it felt satisfying to put Liz in her place. When I returned, Liz's face was red and Tyler looked like he was ready to start a brawl. Everyone else seemed somewhat amused. I took another exaggerated lick of my cone and sat down next to James.

"When did you two start hanging out?" asked Tyler.

"Since the night that you left Emma and me alone on a dirt road to find our own way home. Remember? You were in a rush to go cow tipping with your honey pie, here?" I nodded my head at Liz. Suddenly my smile brightened as I continued. "Actually, I've been wanting to thank you."

Tyler looked confused. "Thank me? For what?"

"You did me a huge favor that night. If you hadn't taken off, leaving James behind to make sure we got home safely, then I never would've gotten to know him. So, thank you."

Tyler muttered something under his breath that I couldn't

understand. His fists were clenched at his side.

"James is my boyfriend," I announced. I hadn't ever called him that before, but I sneaked a sideways glance at him and saw that he was smiling. Tyler, on the other hand, looked furious. I didn't know what his problem was, but I didn't care.

"I'm sure the two of you deserve each other," said Liz nastily. She almost seemed jealous that James and I were together. *Hmm...Did she and James ever date?* I didn't so. She wasn't his type. She was probably just angry because I made her look bad and she had never hidden the fact that she didn't like me.

"Are we going to get ice cream or not?" asked Emma, tugging on Casey's sleeve. She looked bored. She hadn't spoken up earlier, but I knew that Emma enjoyed ice cream as much as I did.

I finished my cone, licking my lips. "Come on, James, let's go."

"Okay. See you guys later."

We stood, but before we could leave, Tyler was in James' face. "I thought I told you to stay away from her." I felt waves of anger coming off of his body.

"I never said I would, man." James shrugged.

Why was Tyler talking to James about me? "Stay out of my business, Tyler. I'll date whoever I want," I stated, getting between them. I didn't understand why Tyler cared so much about who I dated, and since when was he in charge?

"You don't even know this guy, Mike," Tyler proclaimed, pushing me to the side. Only he was used to pushing guys around that were twice my size. I stumbled backwards, losing my balance. Before I landed on my bottom, strong arms reached out and caught me.

"Are you okay?" James set me back on my feet. I could see fire brewing in his now cloudy colored eyes.

Normally I'd make sure Tyler got what was coming to him for pushing me like that, but I didn't want James getting into trouble because of me. He looked like he wanted to tear Tyler's head off. I had to get him out of here. Quickly. Trying to reassure him, I said, "Yeah. I'm fine. It was no big deal." I shrugged, brushing off the incident.

My comment only upset him more. "No big deal? That idiot almost knocked you to the ground. Cousin or not, he had no right." James's fists clenched at his sides. He was ready for a fight, and struggling to keep it together.

"I'm fine. Let's just go," I pleaded, tugging on his arm to make him leave before things got out of hand.

"Wow, that was a close call," muttered Casey. I had little doubt he was trying to force a reaction out of James. "I'd be pissed if someone did that to my girl." He put his arm around Emma and pulled her to him.

"You're so sweet," Emma replied.

"We're leaving," I said, pulling even harder on James' arm.

"Not before he apologizes to you," said James, staring directly at Tyler. "He can't treat you like that and get away with it. It's not cool to push girls around." The muscles in James' face were taut, proving just how serious he was.

I braced myself for an all out fight. I thought for sure Tyler wouldn't apologize, but then he surprised me by saying, "Sorry, Mike. It was an accident. I didn't mean to hurt you. James is right." He nodded. "Hitting girls is wrong. You should ask James what he knows about that. I've heard it's common practice in his neighborhood."

Everyone around us fell silent. The ice cream I ate churned in the pit of my stomach. I felt sick. *What was Tyler talking about?*

"I'd never lay a hand on her," James choked. I felt like everyone was watching us.

"You're doing it now. Look at her arm." Tyler pointed at me.

Everyone moved their eyes to my arm, including me. He

was right; James was squeezing my arm tightly. I hadn't even realized it. He dropped it immediately and it burned bright red for everyone to see. It didn't hurt, but it looked like it did.

James walked away without another word, leaving me standing there, confused. He climbed in his truck and waited. The noise around us returned to normal. People were talking again, eating their ice cream.

I directed my anger and frustration at Tyler. "Stay away from me. And leave James alone." I shoved him with both my hands.

"If you were smart, you'd stay away from him," warned Tyler.

"Fuck you."

I climbed into the truck and shut the door. "Let's go," I said.

James pulled back out onto Main Street. He didn't say a word the whole ride to the farm. Tension hung in the air. I wanted to ask him about what Tyler had said, but I knew he wasn't ready to talk. We pulled into the driveway and I jumped out, ready to move on.

I noticed that James still sat in his truck. "Aren't you coming?" I walked around to his side.

"I don't know if I should?"

"What? It's only 8 o'clock on a Saturday night." He never went home this early.

Reluctantly he climbed out, slowly following me up the porch steps. We sat down on the swing. I carefully took his hand, "What's the matter? You took off and you haven't even said a word to me," I said quietly, my voice filled with concern. I didn't like seeing James so upset. It was obvious Tyler's comments had really affected him.

"Sorry, I just had to get out of there."

"Tyler can be such as ass." I felt the anger building inside of me.

"I have to apologize to you." He lifted my hand and gently

kissed it.

"What on earth do you have to apologize for?" I asked, bewildered.

"For hurting your arm. Does it hurt?" he asked, rubbing it gently.

The truth was I might have a bruise tomorrow, but I didn't want James to know that. He felt bad enough already. "No, it doesn't. So please don't worry." I leaned over and kissed him. He returned my kiss, but I could tell something was wrong. He wasn't into it like he normally was. He was holding a piece of himself back from me. The walls I had partially torn down were back up.

Chapter Sixteen

Dooner

I was lying awake in bed, putting off chores. I still felt uneasy about last night. Every time I closed my eyes, I saw Mikayla's arm almost snap in two because I squeezed it so hard. Also, I heard Tyler's words replaying. Perhaps I had more of my dad in me than I thought. I took a deep breath and let it out. It wasn't true. I wasn't anything like my father. I'd never hurt Mikayla, or any girl for that matter.

I stood up, deciding I needed to be completely honest with Mikayla. I was ready to tell her everything. Things I'd never told anyone. She deserved to know. Suddenly I was skipping around my room, looking for my phone. I found it in a pocket of my discarded jeans and punched in her number. *Damn it*. It went straight to voicemail. I'd have to try again later.

I finished my chores and called her again. I didn't have practice, so I was free to hang out. She still didn't pick up. A thousand different reasons why ran through my head. Was she mad at me for acting standoffish last night? I was contemplating driving over there, when my phone began to ring. I sighed with relief.

"Hey, Baby, how are you?" I asked.

"Terrible," she croaked. Her voice sounded dry and scratchy. I barely recognized it.

Breaking out into a sweat, I asked, "What's wrong?"

"I'm not really sure, but I think I have the flu. I was throwing up all night. And right now I've got the chills." Her voice trembled. I pictured her standing there, shaking, while wearing a sweatshirt and sweatpants even though it was ninety degrees. "I'm sorry, but I can't hang out today."

Suddenly I felt insecure. "I don't care if you're sick. I still want to see you." How was I going to put everything right between us if I couldn't see her? "If this is about last night, I'm sorry. I was just having a bad night. First because Tyler pushed you and then because I thought I'd hurt you."

"This has nothing to do with last night." She paused and I thought I heard dry heaving in the background. "Look James, I gotta go. You can't come over. I'm a mess. And I don't want you to catch whatever I have." She hung up.

I wanted to call back to check on her, but I didn't. A knot formed in my stomach, making me queasy. Maybe I was coming down with whatever Mikayla had. More likely it was because a whole day without her stretched in front of me, causing me anxiety. I'd seen her every day since we started going out. I hoped she got better soon because I didn't know how long I could last without seeing her.

I passed the afternoon writing essays for college applications. I'd received recruiting materials from several top universities, but I'd narrowed it down to three. Penn State, Perdue, and Texas Tech were my top choices, all Division I schools with great football teams and academics. Each year between eighteen and twenty-five new players were signed on with a full scholarship.

Texas Tech was my number one pick—it was the furthest from here. Also I'd been following the team since I was a kid. My dad would sit with me on the couch while we watched them play on TV. I felt the magic when they scored a touchdown. Ever since then, I'd dreamed of being on the team. One of their tight ends was graduating this year. I kept my fingers crossed as I put the finishing touches on my application. I took extra care with this one. My grades were good; my SAT scores were above average, so with any luck my game would be on when the scouts came to check me out.

Since I'd been cooped up in the house all day, I took a drive after dinner. I hopped in Old Faithful, running my hands lovingly over the steering wheel. She was true to her name, just like always, and roared to life when I turned the key. I smiled. Driving around town cleared my head.

Without realizing it, my subconscious had brought me to school. I jumped out and made my way to the middle of the football field. A place where I felt at home. I loved the thrill of the game, the unbeatable adrenaline rush. Looking at the stands, I could almost hear the crowd cheering me on. Football was a part of me.

When I was younger, football was the only connection I had with my dad. We'd watch it together on TV or play catch out in the yard. I used to believe that if I worked hard enough to become the fastest, the smartest, the best football player this town had ever seen, I'd be worthy of my dad's love. But that never happened. Now I was old enough to understand love didn't work that way. I stopped playing for my dad years ago. Now I played just for me.

I marched across the field with a renewed mission and entered the school. It was time I discussed my fate with Coach. I checked his office, but he wasn't there. I went to look for him in the gym. I was almost to the far side and about to give up, when I heard someone come up from behind me. I turned around.

Shit! It was Liz.

"Hi Dooner." She smiled mischievously.

"Hi Liz," I muttered, not masking my displeasure at running into her. It was obvious that she'd been drinking. She had a wine cooler in her hand and she smelled like it wasn't her first one. Seeing her made me miss Mikayla even more.

"Whatjadoing?" she asked, slurring her words.

"I was looking for Coach. I thought he might be in here." I needed to come up with an excuse to get out of here. "I better go check his office again. I bet he's in there, studying the playbook."

"It's the weekend. He's probably at home."

"In any case, I gotta run. See you later." I turned to leave. Liz grabbed my arm, scratching me, and leaving a bright red line on my skin.

"Damn it, Liz. You ought to cut those nails." I rubbed at my arm, but it didn't do any good. The scratch was still there.

"Sorry. I just thought that since we're both here..." She casually shifted her body. I took a step backward to move away from her, not realizing until it was too late that I'd put myself in an even worse situation. Now I was standing in the entrance of the secret make-out corner. "We should make the most of it."

I froze. I didn't want any trouble. I couldn't believe that she was still coming on to me. Sternly, I reminded her, "Liz, I have a girlfriend. And Tyler, remember him? Your boyfriend?

"Yeah, but who cares about all that?" She waved her hand in the air wildly. "It was you and me long before them."

"No, it wasn't." I was still kicking myself for hooking up with her that one time. It was time I set her straight. "We were never an item. And we are never going to be." I turned quickly to walk away, avoiding her grasp this time.

"Whatever, Doonbug." She ran around me and stopped, blocking my path. "Just shut up and fuck me." She reached up and kissed me hard on the mouth. I didn't kiss her back. I felt sick to my stomach. The only lips I ever wanted on mine were Mikayla's.

"Leave me alone, Liz. I'm not interested." I pushed her away and took a giant step back.

"You're an asshole," she shouted. Liz didn't like to be told no. Her angry eyes flashed. She stepped forward and lifted her hand to slap me, but I caught her wrist before she could.

"You're not going to leave another mark on me." I waited until she'd calmed down, "Are you going to behave?" She nodded and I finally let go of her wrist.

Suddenly I sensed an audience. I turned around. Her cheerleading friends, including Emma, had stopped short at the gym door. I wondered how much they saw. By the look on their faces, they'd seen plenty. *Great. How was I going to explain all of this to Mikayla, especially when she didn't even want to see me?*

Chapter Seventeen

Mike

"Ugh," I groaned as I slowly made my way downstairs early Monday morning, leaning heavily on the railing for support. It was the first time since getting sick that I'd left my room. I'd spent all day Sunday either passed out in bed or retching into the toilet. I still felt like hell, but I hoped forcing myself to move around would make me feel better.

"How you feeling?" Pops got up from his chair and came to the bottom of the stairs. He held his hand to me and I gladly took it. He helped me down the last couple of steps.

"A little better...I guess," I answered, trying to sound like I meant it. I didn't want Pops to worry about me.

"You still look pale," he grumbled.

"Thanks." I gave him my best attempt at a dirty look.

"Come sit down." He led me into the kitchen and pulled out my chair. He looked so concerned, I almost felt guilty. "I'll make you some plain toast. That should be okay for your stomach." It felt strange having Pops fix me something to eat. I was the one who normally took care of him.

"Thanks. I am hungry." I hadn't eaten anything since the ice-cream cone on Saturday night, which I threw up. My stomach was empty, but it still hurt; I kept my arm wrapped around my middle.

Pops placed two pieces of dry toast and a small glass of ginger ale in front of me. I took small tentative bites, hoping my stomach wouldn't retaliate.

"You look thin," he commented.

"It's this new diet I'm on. It's called the flu."

"Maybe you are feeling better," he snorted. "I missed your witty comebacks yesterday. It's been too quiet around here." He gave me an encouraging smile.

"Where is everybody?" I asked, looking around the deserted kitchen. More often than not it was just Pops and me. I'd begun to prefer it that way. However, I thought my mom might stick around today to see how I was feeling. I couldn't keep my disappointment from showing.

"Your mom had an early morning meeting. She wanted to be here when you got up, but she didn't think you'd be awake this early. I insisted that if you did wake up, I'd take good care of you. So what do you think? How am I doing?"

I smiled. "You're doing great. Best toast I've ever had." I pushed my almost empty plate away.

"Glad you liked it."

"Is Emma around?" I wanted to know what happened Saturday night after James and I left. What had Tyler meant when he said that hitting girls was a common practice in James' neighborhood?

Pops shook his head. "No, that girl comes and goes. She must think there's a revolving door on this old farmhouse. Why, I've barely seen her since the three of you arrived. She's always running off with her new friends. When she is here, she's either jumping around practicing cheers trying to make this old house fall down, or yapping on that phone of hers."

I laughed, forgetting how much my stomach hurt. "Ouch." I wrapped my arm around my middle even tighter.

"What's wrong?" asked Pops, clearly alarmed by my

reaction.

"Nothing." I tried to act natural, but it was proving to be more and more difficult.

"Are you okay? Maybe this is more than the flu." His forehead creased in concern.

"I'll be fine. Laughing hurt, that's all." Pops still looked worried. I'd have to be more convincing. "Do you have more chores for me to do?" I teased.

"Maybe," he answered gruffly. "But for now, why don't you go sit on the front porch and get some fresh air. You'll be able to see what else needs to be done around here. The last idea you had, about painting a new sign for the vegetable stand, was a good one. I've been meaning to tell you that it's gotten a lot of compliments. Everyone's said how it really grabs their attention when they drive by. Thank you." He smiled proudly.

"You're welcome."

I made it out onto the porch on my own, refusing help. I wanted to put his fears to rest. I smiled and waved at him as I sat down gingerly on the swing. He stood at the door, watching me, for a full minute. My smile never wavered.

"See Pops, I'm fine."

"Humph," he muttered, walking away. He returned a minute later with my phone.

"Here. Your phone rang a thousand times yesterday, if it rang once. Take care of it, would you?" he grouched, attempting to appear tough. If he'd actually been upset, he would've simply shoved it in a drawer until the battery died. The truth was he was turning into an old softie and he didn't want anyone to know.

"Thanks. I promise to take better care of it," I said, playing along.

"I'll be in the house if you need anything."

"Okay." I nodded.

I checked my phone to see what calls I missed. The first

thing I noticed was that James hadn't called even once to see how I was feeling. Paige, however, had called ten times, leaving three messages, each one sounding more urgent than the last.

It was only 7 a.m. in San Francisco, but I called Paige anyway. "Hi, Paige. What's up? Is everything okay?"

"Where the hell have you been? I tried to reach you all day yesterday."

"Sorry, I was sick," I answered weakly. I wasn't feeling very good at the moment. My stomach was cramping. *Maybe the toast wasn't such a good idea after all.*

"Oh, sorry," she said sheepishly. "Are you feeling better today?"

"No, not really." My free arm was still wrapped tightly around my middle.

"What's the matter?"

"I think I have the flu," I moaned. I wanted to tell her what happened at Blondie's, but I was too sick to get the words out. My stomach felt like it was being stabbed with a sharp knife.

"Shit. Mike, that's bad. And now I feel even worse, because I have bad news of my own. That's why I've been trying to call you...I....I..."

"Whatever it is, hurry up and spit it out, before I puke." I wiped the sweat off my forehead with the back of my hand.

"Promise you won't hate me?"

I didn't have time for this. "Of course I won't hate you. But stop stalling and just tell me. Pops won't like it if his front porch is covered in my breakfast."

"Okay, okay." She took a deep breath and continued all at once. "I'm so sorry, but I can't come to see you like we planned. I know it's short notice. But after we spoke, I crashed the front end of my parents' car. I was backing out of the driveway, looking behind me to make sure I wasn't going to run anyone over, when I turned my wheel too sharply. I clipped the mailbox with the front of the car. My parents are making me use the money from my plane ticket to pay for the repairs. You wouldn't believe the damage—the whole front bumper's torn off."

I laughed, remembering too late how much it hurt.

"It's not funny," she yelled.

"Yes, it is. Only you could destroy the front of the car while backing up."

"I miss you," she admitted.

"I miss you too."

"I'm so depressed that I won't be there for your eighteenth birthday. That's the day I was supposed to arrive. I'm really sorry I screwed up."

"It's okay. You'll have to save up your money and come to visit me another time. Maybe you can come for a few days over Christmas break and experience real snow."

"Yeah, that sounds like fun. You promise you're not mad?"

"I promise. But I do have to go."

Two seconds after I hung up, I was leaning over the railing, puking up the toast along with a lot of disgusting green bile.

Feeling a little better, I sat back down on the swing. With the pain in my stomach temporarily gone, the wheels in my brain started to turn. *Why hadn't James called me? Was he upset with me because Tyler made a stupid comment that I hadn't even understood? Was he planning on breaking up with me?* I thought about how he wasn't himself after we returned from Blondie's that night. He was distant and broody. My temperature rose, as I grew angrier by the minute. Suddenly I stood up. I couldn't just sit here. I had to do something before I lost James for good.

Chapter Eighteen

Dooner

I was in the locker room changing after practice when suddenly there was a lot of commotion. From around the corner someone shouted angrily, "Hey, can't you read, this is the guys' locker room."

"No wait, she's here to see me," another voice answered. "This hot little number's going to suck my cock, huh sweetie?" That caused all the guys to shout and whistle. *What the hell's going on?* I quickly pulled my shorts on.

"Not a chance in Hell, you've got nothing there," a female voice said, laughing. I'd recognize that voice anywhere. *What's she doing here?* The room instantly filled with loud cheers. *This isn't going to end well.*

"Hold on, bitch. It'll only take a second. I just got out of the cold shower. I wasn't expecting you...so soon," he said. My heart pounded as I rushed over. What was Mikayla thinking, walking into a locker room filled with half-naked testosterone-ridden football players? I had to get her out of here before there was trouble.

I stopped when I saw her standing there with her hands on her hips and her crazy hair fanning out all around her.

Damn, she's beautiful.

Tyler arrived at the same moment I did, looking like he shared some of my anxiety at her being here. "What the hell, Mike," he said, wrapping his towel tightly around his waist. "You can't just come barging in here."

"Really? Because it looks like I just did," she said, fire behind her eyes. *What is this all about?*

"Well, you have to get out. Now!" He tried to maneuver her back toward the door. I felt my anger build. He'd better not even think about shoving her again. I'd lose it this time if he so much as laid a finger on her. I took a step toward them.

Without warning, Tyler's towel loosened and fell to the ground before he could catch it. "Damn it, Mikayla," he shouted over the loud laughter that erupted all around. His face was beet red. "Out." He bent over to pick up his towel and wrapped it around his waist again.

"Please, like I haven't seen it before." She shrugged, making Tyler furious. "I'm not leaving here until I've said what I've come here to say." She stood her ground.

Tyler sighed. "This is not the place." For once I agreed with him.

The locker room had grown silent. All the guys were standing around, watching and waiting to see what would happen next.

"Just shut up, Tyler, and listen," she shouted, taking a step closer to him. "Don't you ever put your hands on me again." She took another step closer. Her eyes were dark; you could barely make out her pupils. "And don't interfere in my relationship with James." She paused before adding, "You got that?"

"Yeah, loud and clear," he muttered, sounding like a scolded child. If the scene hadn't been so personal, I might have enjoyed witnessing Tyler humbled. "Finished?"

"Almost. I also came to talk to you," she said, acknowledging me for the first time. The team also shifted their focus. I braced myself for what she had to say.

Her eyes were still dark, but I detected a hint of sadness in them. "What kind of boyfriend are you?" she questioned. She continued without letting me answer. "You let this giant oaf scare you away?" She nodded at Tyler, and several guys snickered. "And worse, I told you I was sick and you didn't even call me once to see how I was feeling. Some boyfriend you turned out to be. Ugh," she groaned, dropping her hands from her hips and wrapping her arms around her middle. Without another word, she spun on her heel and left. I stood there in shock.

As soon as the show was over, the noise in the locker room increased, everyone buzzing about what just happened. Finally, I snapped out of it.

I took off after her wearing only my shorts. "Mikayla," I yelled, looking all around. Where could she have gone? Why did she disappear like that? *She didn't even let me explain.*

She wasn't in the hall. *Can she have darted into the girls' locker room?* I had my hand on the door when it opened.

"Dooner. What a surprise," feigned Liz. "Was that a love quarrel I just witnessed?"

"Is she in there?" I asked.

"Yeah, she's in there. And so is the rest of the cheerleading squad. There's no chance in Hell that you're getting by me." She stuck out her chest as she moved to stand directly in front of the door, blocking it. "What did you do now to upset that poor girl?" When I didn't respond, Liz continued, "Well, whatever it was, it made her run straight for the toilet. Right now she's puking her guts out." She laughed.

I didn't find any of this funny. I'd noticed that Mikayla was a little flushed. I just thought it was because she was so worked up. Maybe she wasn't feeling well again.

"Let me by, Liz," I said through clenched teeth.

"No." She smiled devilishly. "And if you try I'll be sure to tell Mike about our little rendezvous last night by the bleachers."

"Go ahead. There's nothing to tell."

"Are you sure about that? I was crying when the girls found me in the gym. You kissed me and when I didn't kiss you back you had a hard time taking no for an answer. They saw you grabbing my wrist and twisting it. Why, I think Emma said she saw the scratch on your arm that I gave you when I tried to get away." Instinctively I looked down at my arm, making me appear guilty. The mark stood out brightly against my skin. However, it didn't happen the way Liz was implying. She knew it too. She was after something.

"What do you want, Liz?" I asked, growing impatient with her games.

"You know what I want," she said, running her red painted fingernails down my bare chest. I shivered in horror. "I know you want me too. You're wasting your time with that bitch in there." She pointed behind her. "She's not like you and me."

"Get it through your head. I'm not interested in you. And I never will be."

"We'll see," Liz said, sounding sickeningly sweet.

I was about to respond when Tyler came sauntering down the hall.

"Hey, baby." He made a bee-line over to Liz, sticking his tongue halfway down her throat. It looked more like a perverted dental exam, than a kiss. I shook my head in disgust.

Tyler finally came up for air. "What's going on?" he asked, eyeing me suspiciously.

Liz answered, "I'm guarding the door. You'll never believe this, but your crazy cousin, Mike, went running into the girls' locker room. Dooner thinks he can just break the door down and go in after her." She rolled her eyes.

"Really?"

"That's all you're going to say?" asked Liz in utter surprise.

"Yeah." He shrugged.

"You have to stop him," Liz pleaded.

"No, I don't."

Tyler looked at me and continued. "I've changed my mind. You and Mike deserve each other. I was just trying to look out for her, but apparently she can handle things herself."

"Gee, thanks, man," I said sarcastically.

"Come on, let's get out of here. I have some steam I need to blow off." He grabbed her ass as they walked toward the gym. I had few doubts about where they were headed. She looked over her shoulder at me one last time before they were out of sight.

With Liz finally out of the way, I could go in and see what was wrong with Mikayla. I opened the door, just as Emma was bringing her out. She could barely stand up.

I gasped. There was definitely something wrong with her. She was as white as a ghost. I'd never seen her look so pale and weak.

"What happened?"

"She has the flu, you jackass." Emma gave me a dirty look.

"Here, let me help." I picked Mikayla up easily, cradling her in my arms. She was light as a feather. Holding her, I also realized that she had a high fever. Her skin felt hot against my bare chest. My skin always heated up when she touched me, but not like this. This was different. "I don't think this is the flu, I think it's something more than that. She's been throwing up for two days now. And she's burning up."

"Put me down," she murmured weakly without even putting up a fight. I gently brushed her hair back. She couldn't even hold up her head; it rested against my shoulder. *If anything happens to her...*

"What should we do?" Emma asked worriedly.

"I don't know. We could call someone for help."

"Hey, maybe my mom's still here," Emma said hopefully. "She came in early for a meeting. I can go to her room and see."

"Okay, but hurry."

It felt like Emma was gone forever. I paced back and forth; Mikayla barely moved in my arms. Finally she returned with their mom. I felt relief at seeing her. She'd know what to do.

"What's she doing here?" her mom asked, frowning. "She's supposed to be home in bed."

"All I know is that she came bursting into the girls' locker room looking really sick. She ran straight for the toilets and started throwing up. It sounded awful." Emma cringed.

A moan escaped Mikayla's dry lips. She didn't even have the energy to speak.

"I'm so glad you're here, Mrs. Mooney. I'm really worried about her. She's burning up with fever."

Mrs. Mooney gently placed her palm on Mikayla's forehead, letting out a deep sigh. She was visibly distraught. "You're absolutely right, she is hot. She's been sick since Saturday night." She counted on her fingers. "I think I better take her directly to the doctor." Mrs. Mooney quickly took charge. "Emma, run to the nurse's office and get an ice pack to cool her down. James, if you could carry Mike out to my car, I'd appreciate it. I have to run back to my classroom and grab my purse. We'll meet at my car. You know which car is mine, right?"

"Yes, the blue Audi S4 convertible."

"Right. See you in a minute." She turned and headed back down the hall. She wasn't running, but she sure was walking fast.

I had to walk a little slower. I didn't want to jostle Mikayla too much. She'd begun to whimper softly in my arms. I pushed open the door to the outside with my shoulder and stepped out into the humidity. Sweat beaded on her forehead. Mikayla looked small and frail in my arms; I felt so helpless. I located Mrs. Mooney's car just as Emma jogged up with the ice pack.

The convertible top was down, so I carefully laid her in the backseat. She curled up into a ball, moaning again. Emma placed the ice pack on her forehead and she sighed.

Mrs. Mooney caught up with us. "I see how she got here." She pointed at Mikayla's grandfather; he sat in his truck, a few feet away. He noticed us too, and came running over as quickly as he could.

"What happened to her?" he asked, surprised.

"I don't know, Dad. Why don't you tell me?" She snapped, accusing him.

"Well, she was all fired up to talk to Tyler." He didn't even mention my name, but he gave me a look that said he knew I was part of this too. "She said she had unfinished business that couldn't wait." Mrs. Mooney glared. "She convinced me to bring her here," he confessed, sheepishly. He took a handkerchief out of his back pocket and wiped his brow. "I knew I never should've let her talk me into it." It was obvious that I wasn't the only one who'd fallen under Mikayla's spell.

"We'll straighten it out later. I don't have time right now. I need to get her to the doctor."

"Is she going to be okay?" he asked, his voice suddenly sounding years older.

"I hope so." She nodded at her dad, dismissing him as she opened her car door and slid behind the wheel. "Thanks for your help, James," she added.

"No problem. I'll come by later to see how she's feeling."

Mr. Jenkins and I stood and watched until we couldn't see the bright blue car anymore. Finally I said, "Thanks for not bringing up my name."

"Don't mention it, kid. I know the two of you will work things out. She doesn't say it, but I can tell she really cares about you."

I smiled. Mr. Jenkins was pretty cool for an old guy. "You know it's not your fault that she's sick."

Mr. Jenkins kicked the ground with the toe of his boot. "I

know. But I didn't help any by driving her here today. I should've insisted she stay home."

"Mikayla has a mind of her own. Something tells me she would've found a way here no matter what." I chuckled.

Mr. Jenkins chuckled too. "Don't I know it? That's why I brought her here myself, figured it was the lesser of two evils. And look how things turned out." He shook his head. "She takes after her mother, you know. Stubborn as can be. Good luck to you, kid." He patted me on my bare back. I'd forgotten that I was still shirtless.

"Thanks, Mr. Jenkins. Looks like I better head back in and finish getting changed."

"Good idea, son."

Later that evening, I knew something was wrong as soon as I pulled into Mikayla's driveway. Mrs. Mooney's car was gone and Mikayla wasn't waiting for me on the porch. I raced up the porch steps two at a time. Knocking loudly on the front door, I waited for it to open.

"Hiya James." Mr. Jenkins, opened the door. His face had a serene look. It couldn't be good news.

He opened the door wider and stepped out onto the porch. "Come on, let's sit down a minute."

I didn't sit on the swing like usual. It hurt to even look at it. Instead I chose to sit in the empty rocking chair next to Mr. Jenkins.

"How bad is it?" I asked tentatively.

"She has appendicitis." He paused for a second, and then continued. "Everything should be okay, though. She made it to the hospital before it burst. She's in surgery now. My daughter Sarah, Mike's mom, is going to call as soon as she has news to report."

It took me a second to process what he'd said. "Wow. I didn't see that coming. I'm glad she made it to the hospital in time. I just hope everything goes okay." My stomach was tied in knots. *She has to be okay.*

Surprising me, Mr. Jenkins reached out his hand, covered in age spots, and lightly touched my shoulder. "I'm sure she's going to be just fine. But if you want to stay until Sarah calls, you're more than welcome to. I'm sure it'll be any minute now."

"Thanks." I nodded.

"No problem. It'll help pass the time. I started to ask you this once before. Are you any good at crossword puzzles?"

"I don't know. I've never done them before," I said honestly.

"Well, just so you know, Mike's real good at them. I can't say the same about her sister. Or her cousins, for that matter."

I chuckled. "I sure I'm not as smart as Mikayla, but I'll give it a try."

"That a boy," he replied, pulling a crossword out of his front pocket. He pulled a pen out from behind his ear, making me grin. "Do you know who won Super Bowl XX?"

"Yes, and I'm sure you do too. Is that even one of the questions?" I asked, pointing to the crossword.

"Maybe?" He laughed.

"The Chicago Bears," I replied.

"Right, you are." He filled in an answer. "It's on football trivia. I thought it would be appropriate."

I nodded with a smile. "Cool."

"I've been saving it. Mike's smart, but the truth is she doesn't know a thing about football." He laughed and his eyes crinkled. It was obvious he cared deeply about her.

"Yeah, football isn't really her thing. I hope she'll come to a game," I added wistfully.

"I'm sure she will. Lately she's been slipping in questions about how the game is played while we tend to the garden. I wonder why that is?" He winked.

We spent the next half hour working on the puzzle. Like him, I knew all the answers. We were both equally passionate about the game. When the phone finally rang, it made us both jump. Mr. Jenkins practically knocked over his chair in his haste to answer it.

Suddenly the porch felt empty and eerily quiet. My heart pounded, wondering what was taking so long. Was it bad news?

"James," Mr. Jenkins called out from inside the house.

I stood and shouted through the screen door, "Yeah?"

"Come on in here."

I cautiously entered, not knowing what to expect. I walked through to the kitchen where Mr. Jenkins was talking on a phone attached to the wall. "Yeah?" I asked nervously.

Mr. Jenkins held the phone out to me. "Here. My daughter wants to talk to you."

"Okay." I took the phone.

"I'll be out on the porch," Mr. Jenkins said and left.

"Hello?" I said, hesitantly.

"James?"

"Yes..."

"This is Mrs. Mooney. I wanted to let you know that Mike's going to be fine." I let out an audible sigh of relief. "Thanks for helping today. I don't know how I would've gotten her into the car if it hadn't been for you."

Guilt rushed over me. It was partly my fault that she came to school when she should've been home in bed. "You don't need to thank me. It was the least I could do. I'm so happy that she's going to be all right."

"She'll make a complete recovery. However, she'll be in the hospital for a couple of days and I'm sure she'd love it if you visited."

"I'll be there tomorrow." I had to see for myself that she was going to be okay. Plus I had a lot of making up to do.

"Wonderful."

"Thanks, Mrs. Mooney."

"No, James, thank you."

"Bye," I said.

"Goodnight," replied Mikayla's mom. I carefully replaced the phone on its hook.

* * * *

After our second practice was over, I quickly showered and got dressed. I couldn't wait to see Mikayla. I jogged out to the parking lot where Old Faithful was waiting. Absentmindedly I tossed my stuff into the back. It was 5:45 p.m. Visiting hours ended at 8, so Mikayla and I had an hour and a half to spend together.

I put my key in the ignition and turned it. Nothing happened. *Shit!* I banged the steering wheel. *I don't have time for this.* I tried again. Still nothing.

Feeling anxiety building, I took a deep breath. Talking sweetly to Old Faithful, I said, "Come on, girl. Don't do this to me. I have an important date I can't miss." I rubbed the dashboard. "You've never let me down before. I know you can do it." I closed my eyes and turned the key one more time. Complete silence.

"Damn it," I shouted.

I jumped out and popped open the hood. I'd been tinkering around with engines for as long as I could remember. However, it didn't require a mechanical engineering degree to figure out that the battery was dead. When I bought Old Faithful from my uncle he told me the battery would run for about two years, and that was two and a half years ago. I sighed in frustration, slamming the hood down. I'd be lucky if I made it to the hospital before visiting hours were over.

I didn't have a lot of options. I asked around for a jump, but I didn't have jumper cables and neither did anyone else. I could've walked to the local garage, but that wasn't practical. It would've taken a long time and then I would've been stuck carrying a heavy battery all the way back to my truck. I could've called a tow truck, but that was too expensive. Time was ticking. Finally I pulled out my phone. "Hello. Mr. Jenkins?"

"Yes?"

"It's me, James. I need your help."

Ten minutes later, Mr. Jenkins pulled into the parking lot. He gave me a jump and then followed me to Tom's garage in case the charge didn't last long enough to get there.

"Thanks, Mr. Jenkins. I really appreciate you helping me out like this," I said, making it to the garage.

"No problem, son. Go and see if Tom has a new battery. I'll stick around until you're all set."

"Thanks."

I found Tom, the owner, underneath a car changing its oil. I cleared my throat loudly. "Hey, Tom, is that you?"

"Yeah," he said, rolling out from underneath. He wiped his hands on a rag. "What can I do for you, Dooner?"

"Old Faithful ran out of juice. I need to get a new battery for her. Do you have one in stock?"

"I don't know. I'll go and see. Are you planning on changing it yourself? I'm a little backed up. I couldn't get to it until maybe sometime tomorrow afternoon at the earliest."

"Yeah, I can do it as long as you have one."

"Okay. I'll be right back."

I kept checking my phone for the time. I couldn't believe it was 6:30 already when Tom came back out.

"Here you are," he said, handing me the battery.

"Thanks so much. Can I pay you tomorrow? I don't have enough cash on me since I wasn't expecting to need a new battery and all."

"No problem. Stop by any time. I'll be here all day. Help yourself to whatever tools you need to get her running again. Just make sure you win the first big game of the year."

"I'll do my best." The whole town would be disappointed if I didn't play in that game. "Thanks, Tom," I said.

"Okay. I gotta get back to work." He slid back under the car he was working on.

Mr. Jenkins helped me install the new battery. It was easier and quicker with his help. I could see why Mikayla and him hit if off, despite the fact that they'd probably both deny it if anyone asked them. The truth was they were a lot a like.

"Get in and let's see if she starts," said Mr. Jenkins from under the hood.

I turned the key and gave her gas. She immediately roared to life. "Woo-hoo," I shouted.

Mr. Jenkins put the hood back down. "She's as good as new." He moved out of the way. "You better go if you're going to make it."

"Thanks, Mr. Jenkins. I really appreciate you helping me out tonight. I owe you one," I quickly jumped out and shook his hand.

"No need to thank me. Just say hello to my granddaughter for me when you see her." He winked.

"Will do." I jumped back in my truck and drove away.

It was going to be a close one. It was a thirty-minute drive to the hospital and it was already 7:15. I drove as quickly as I could without getting a speeding ticket.

I pushed open the main door of the hospital at exactly 8:00 p.m. I rushed over to the reception desk where a scary Amazon-looking receptionist sat. "Hi. Can you please tell me which room Mikayla Mooney is in?"

She stared disapprovingly at me. I was covered in sweat and grease from changing the battery. "No young man, I cannot. Visiting hours are over. See the sign? They end at 8 p.m. and right now it is 8:01. You'll have to come back tomorrow morning."

I felt all the air go out of me, like a flat tire. "Yeah, but I really need to see her tonight. She's expecting me. I won't stay but a minute, I promise." *Mikayla won't forgive me this time.*

"Those are the rules," she said determinedly.

I couldn't just give up and go home. I was looking for a way to sneak past the receptionist, who was watching me closely, when I spotted Mrs. Mooney getting off the elevator.

"Hi, Mrs. Mooney. I'm here to see Mikayla. I would've been here sooner, but my truck wouldn't start," I said all at once.

"Oh, James." She frowned. "I'd take you up to her room, but the nurse just kicked me out, visiting hours are over."

"You're her mother, surely you can get me in to see her," I said, sounding desperate.

"I wish I could. Apparently they're strict here about the patients getting enough rest." My shoulders sagged. "You'll have to wait to see her until tomorrow."

"How is she?"

"She's okay. She wants to go home, but the doctors are keeping her one more night. As long as everything's fine, she can go home in the morning."

"Cool." I smiled brightly.

"Can you keep a secret?" she asked, putting her arm through mine. I nodded. "Tomorrow is Mike's eighteenth birthday, which you probably already know."

"Yeah," I replied. Mikayla had only mentioned her birthday in passing, but I had taken special note of it.

We had arrived in the parking garage and I could see Mrs. Mooney's Audi up ahead. "Well, I'm planning a surprise party for her, since she'll be getting out of the hospital."

"Okay," I answered slowly. I wasn't so sure that Mikayla liked parties or surprises. I thought back to the day that we met at the road party, and then a few days later when I showed up unannounced on her front porch. She hadn't been overjoyed on either of those occasions. I shook my head and smiled. Sometimes things had a way of working out.

Chapter Nineteen

Mike

"Finally," I said, standing, as my mom sauntered into my hospital room. I'd been dressed and ready to go home since 7 a.m.—it was already after 10. "Let's go."

"Hi to you too, honey." My mom chuckled. "You might as well sit back down. I have to stop by the nurse's station and sign your papers. I came in here first to say good morning." She bent down and kissed the top of my head.

"It's barely still morning and it certainly isn't good," I grouched.

"Sounds like someone's feeling better," my mom commented on her way out the door.

While I waited, an orderly came in with a wheel chair. "I got your ride here, miss."

"Thanks," I mumbled. I couldn't help but remember how James had easily picked me up and carried me in his strong arms. I sighed, wishing he were here now instead of this cold wheelchair. Then, just as quickly, I remembered how he hadn't even bothered to call, or come to see me.

My mom pulled the car around. "Where's Pops?" I asked once I was settled in. I was sure he'd come to pick me up. He hadn't been to visit me either. I was only in the hospital for less than 48 hours, but still I thought he'd come, today being my birthday and all. I couldn't believe how sad I felt that he wasn't here. I really missed him.

"He hates hospitals." She gave me an apologetic smile.

"I know the feeling," I mumbled.

It was a quiet ride back to the farm. I didn't feel like talking. I was exhausted. I hadn't slept at all in the hospital, with the monitors going off every few minutes, and the lights in the hallway on all night long. Also, I was depressed. Neither Pops nor James had visited me in the hospital. Paige wasn't coming to town. And worst of all, my mom hadn't even wished me a happy birthday.

How could she have forgotten? I slumped against the window in the passenger seat and looked out at the passing scenery without really seeing it. In the past, birthdays had always been a big deal in my family. My dad went out of his way to make sure that they were extra special. My throat tightened. I thought that signing and dating my discharge papers would have reminded her that today was my eighteenth birthday, but I guessed not. I closed my eyes to hold back the tears.

Finally I opened them and saw Pop-Pop's house up head. A warm feeling spread through me; it felt good to be almost home. When she turned the corner, the first thing I noticed was James' truck in the driveway. A smile spread across my face. My aunt's truck was there too.

My mom parked. I took a moment to process the scene on the front porch. There were two big banners stretched across the front. That looked like Emma's handiwork: "Welcome home, Mike," and "Happy 18th birthday!" A small group waited expectantly. It was the same group that had gathered here the day we arrived—well, almost. James hadn't been here then. A different feeling settled in my stomach today upon seeing them. Today I wasn't angry and resentful. I was happy.

I smiled from ear to ear.

Slowly I turned to face my mom. "Thanks." I wanted to say more, but I couldn't get the words out. I was too choked up.

"You're welcome. You didn't really think I'd forget your birthday, did you?"

I didn't answer, but it was written all over my face.

"I did give birth to you, you know." She laughed, making me feel better. "How'd I do? Did I get it right?" she asked, pointing toward the front porch.

"You did great, Mom, thanks." I reached over and gave her a hug.

"Well, you better go enjoy your guests," she said, pointing. "They're waiting for you."

I smiled brightly as I stepped out of the car. All at once everyone started singing "Happy Birthday" while Emma came out onto the porch, carrying a cake with eighteen candles.

"Make a wish," my mom said, putting her arm around me. We stepped onto the porch.

"My wish already came true." I looked around, one by one, at the people I loved until my gaze finally came to rest on James. Instantly my face grew warm.

"There must be something," my mom insisted.

I blushed even redder. I could only think of one thing I didn't already have. And it wasn't something you found at a store. I quickly took a deep breath and blew out the candles before anyone could read my mind. All the candles went out. Did that mean my wish was going to come true? The porch erupted in claps and cheers.

My mom appeared with a knife and a stack of paper plates. "Who wants cake? It's Mike's favorite, yellow cake with chocolate frosting a la mode." My mom cut the cake while Emma scooped ice cream. I served it and personally thanked everyone for coming.

Pops was at the top of my list. "Here," I said, handing him

a piece of cake and leaping into his arms for a big hug, almost smashing the cake between us. Normally I wasn't into physical contact, but right now it was exactly what the doctor ordered. Pops hugged me back as tightly as my recent surgery would allow.

"Hey now, girl. What's gotten into you?" he asked, finally releasing me. "Did they do more than take out your appendix in the hospital?" He pulled on one of my curls. Pops was like me; showing emotions wasn't something we were good at.

"I'm sorry. It's just that I'm so happy to be home." I smiled. Nowhere was my home now. This old farm house, surrounded by my family and James, was were I belonged.

Pops returned my smile with one of his own. "It makes my day to hear you say that. I didn't realize how lonely I was until you moved in and started stomping around and banging cupboard doors. It sure was quiet the past two days."

"That reminds me, you didn't even come to see me while I was in the hospital."

"Yeah, sorry about that, kid. I don't like hospitals." He shivered.

"Me either. I don't blame you for not wanting to come," I said, forgiving him.

"That's not the only reason I didn't visit you. The truth is I was feeling guilty about driving you to school that day. I'm real sorry I did. I never should've let you convince me." Pops looked ashamed.

"Oh, Pops, it's not your fault," I gushed, wanting to make him feel better. "I would've gone whether you drove me or not." I instinctively touched my side, remembering. "And I would've ended up in the hospital regardless."

"It is your fault that she's so stubborn though." My mom laughed, coming up behind us—she didn't mention that she was also stubborn. I guessed it ran in the family. "Mike, don't forget about the rest of your guests." She nodded to everyone else.

"I won't." I left them to continue making my rounds.

"Hi, Aunt Carol. Thanks for coming."

"Oh, darling, I'm just glad you're okay." She gave me a tight squeeze.

"Happy birthday, cuz," said Austin.

"Thanks." I gave him a quick hug. I didn't want anyone to feel left out.

Tyler came over when he saw me talking to his mom and his brother. He'd been sitting with Emma. She stood up to carry the ice cream back inside before it melted. James held the door open for her. "You sure are one tough girl, Mike." Tyler squeezed my shoulders. "First you have the guts to come barging into the guys' locker room." He laughed.

"I'm glad you can laugh about it now," I commented.

"What else can I do?" He shrugged. *Maybe Tyler isn't so bad.* "And then you then get appendicitis and make a full recovery. You make it look easy."

"Thanks, I guess." I chuckled. I wasn't really sure how to respond. It did, however, feel like there was a compliment in there somewhere.

"I'm sorry I pushed you the other night." I nodded, accepting his apology. This one felt real, unlike the apology he gave me because James made him. "And the truth is—you could do worse." He glanced over at James who sat nearby, talking to Pops. "I promise not to interfere again."

"Good." It seemed Tyler and I had reached an agreement. Things really were falling into place here, making my smile widen.

"You have presents to open," my mom interrupted, carrying out a small stack. My face flushed.

"Open our gift first, sweetie," said Aunt Carol. "It's the one in the blue wrapping paper. I have to get the boys home soon so that they can get ready for this afternoon's practice."

"Oh, sure," I stuttered. I forgot that James would have to leave soon. My smile faltered slightly. I hadn't even made it around to talk to him yet.

I carefully unwrapped the presents. My aunt gave me a hideous short-sleeve purple blouse that I'd never wear, but I smiled and thanked her anyway. Pops gave me a quirky card that made me laugh, with a check inside. Next I opened a raspberry-colored graphic T-shirt from Emma that I couldn't wait to try on. The last present in the pile was from my mom, a jean jacket with three quarter sleeves, and a really fabulous art book of the paintings in the Louvre. My eyes teared up as I flipped through the pages. I recognized it as a final gift from my dad. Paris was the last place he traveled to for his job.

"Thank you," I said shyly. I was touched by everyone's thoughtfulness. I hadn't expected anything. Having them all here was more than enough.

Suddenly James spoke up, "I didn't forget your present. It's just that you'll have to wait until later." It was the first words he'd spoken to me since I'd come bursting into the locker room.

"Okay," I answered slowly, trying to guess at his cryptic message. I wondered if my birthday wish was going to come true.

"I thought I'd come by after dinner, like I always do. It needs to be dark out, in order for the present to work."

What did that mean? Confused, I said, "Sure. That's fine."

Aunt Carol, Tyler, and Austin wished me well and left. Pops mumbled about going inside to sit in his chair while my mom and Emma carried leftover cake inside. It felt a little rehearsed, but I didn't care. James and I were finally alone.

Immediately I went over and sat next to him on the swing. Finally it was out turn to talk. I didn't really know where to begin. He reached out and lightly stroked my cheek with his fingertips, causing goose bumps to arise on my skin. My body responded to his lightest touch.

"I'm sorry," he whispered. "I know you're upset with me and I don't blame you. You're right, I should've called on

Sunday night to see how you were feeling. I wanted to, but I honestly thought you didn't want to see me anymore after what happened at Blondie's. Then you showed up in the locker room giving me hell, and I realized I'd been wrong. I tried to make it up to you by visiting you in the hospital, but my truck chose that exact moment to die. Pops had to give me a jump and then he helped me install a new battery. By the time I got to the hospital, visiting hours were over. I ran into your mom as she was leaving and she invited me over today. She said she thought it would make you happy if I came. So...are you...happy?"

I looked down at our intertwined hands. "You could've called." I wasn't angry, but it still hurt.

"I did, but your phone went directly into voice mail. Then I remembered that cell phones aren't allowed in hospitals." He paused. "Can you forgive me for being such a dumbass?"

My heart softened. It was nothing more than a misunderstanding. And it wasn't his fault his truck broke down. However, I didn't want to give in too quickly. "I forgive you, but I'm not happy *yet*," I said.

He raised his eyebrows. "Would this help?" he asked in a husky voice, as he lowered his head and lightly brushed his lips against mine. My heart completely melted. I put my arms around his neck and pulled him closer to me. I had missed the feel of his lips the past few days. My heart knew I didn't really have a choice but to forgive him. James made me happy.

Suddenly my mom came out onto the porch, making more noise than was necessary. James and I pulled apart. I was sure my face was as red as his. My parents had always been affectionate with each other, holding hands and kissing in front of us. We weren't doing anything more than that, but somehow it felt like we were. "Okay, Mike, it's time to rest."

James stood and wiped his hands on his jeans. "I have to go, anyway. I have practice. I'll come back later, after dinner, if that's still okay?" He glanced nervously at my mom. She nodded her head in approval. "See you later." He bent over and kissed the top of my head.

I climbed the stairs to my room and lay down on my bed. I sighed. It felt good to be home. The sleepless night and the emotional day had worn me out. I quickly fell asleep.

I awoke two hours later, feeling well rested. I stretched and went into the bathroom to freshen up. Looking in the mirror, I got an idea. I owed James a self-portrait.

I gathered my art supplies and returned to the bathroom. I stared at my reflection in the mirror for a full five minutes before touching my pencil to the paper. I wanted to get it just right. I started with my eyes, big and brown. I was using a charcoal pencil so I shaded them in to match the depth. There was nothing noteworthy about my nose. It was just in the middle of my face. Next I drew my high cheekbones, shading them in to look like I was blushing. My lips were full. I drew the corners upturned slightly to form a smile. I was always happy when I was with James. My chin was slightly pointed, which was the feature I liked the least about my face. Of course my hair curled in every direction and completely filled in the rest of the paper. When I finished, I stood back and inspected my work. Feeling satisfied, I returned to my room. I carefully sprayed my masterpiece, so that it wouldn't smudge and set it on the dresser to dry. Later, I'd put it in a frame to give to James.

After dinner, I joined Pops in the family room to help him with his crossword puzzle, passing time until James arrived. "Are you sure you're feeling up to answering a few questions?" he asked, eyeing me suspiciously.

"I'm sure," I said, sitting down.

"Did you know, your boyfriend is also good at puzzles?" He grinned.

"You didn't?" I exclaimed.

"What? He didn't mind." I raised my eyebrows. "He's smart. He's going to go places, that boy. I like him."

"Enough, Pops." He was embarrassing me. "Ask me a hard one."

"Okay. You asked for it." He looked over the page. "Author Edgar Allen____?"

"Poe. That was easy."

"Angel's topper?"

"Halo."

Before he could ask me another question, I heard James pull in and I jumped up. "I just remembered I left something upstairs."

Pops chuckled. "Slow down before you get yourself all worked up," he demanded. "I don't want you getting sick on us again."

It warmed my heart the way Pops looked out for me. "Don't worry, I promise not to overdo it." I walked slowly out of the room.

"I'll make sure he doesn't go anywhere," he called after me.

I smiled. "Tell him I'll be right down."

From upstairs, I heard James knock on the screen door. When I came down the stairs, James and Pops were talking in the front hall. My face lit up when I saw him. He was looking as handsome as ever, wearing a plaid button-down shirt with the sleeves rolled up, jeans, and cowboy boots. His sandy hair was tousled and his green eyes were clear and bright.

"Ah, to be young again," Pops said wistfully, observing us. "You two going out on the porch?"

"Yeah."

"Have fun," he said, returning to his chair.

We walked outside and sat down on the swing. I held my package out to him.

"What's this?" he asked, taking it from me. "I thought it was your birthday. I'm supposed to be giving *you* a gift?"

"Just open it."

He tore it open. His eyes went wide and turned a deeper

shade of green. He studied it closely before commenting. I held my breath, waiting. Quietly, his voice full of awe and admiration, he said, "I love it. I can't believe you drew this for me. It's beautiful, just like you. Thank you."

"You're welcome."

"It's the nicest gift anyone's ever given me." His eyes proved that he was telling the truth.

"I'm glad you like it."

"I have a present for you too, but we have to wait until it gets dark out."

"Why?" I asked, intrigued.

"I can't tell you. That would ruin the surprise. And I thought you liked surprises."

"I hate surprises," I stated emphatically.

"Really? You seemed to enjoy your surprise party today," he gently reminded me.

"I did, didn't I?" I laughed. "Okay, maybe I don't hate surprises. I just hate waiting."

"Don't worry, it'll be worth it," he reassured me.

We passed the evening hanging out on the porch, talking and enjoying each other's company. I snuggled into the crook of his arm, fitting perfectly. I had a hard time remembering why I thought my old life back in San Francisco was so great. I had everything I needed right here. Eventually dusk turned to darkness.

James stood and said, "Stay here. I gotta get something out of my truck."

He returned with a rectangle shaped present that looked like it might be a book and a large black case. "I hope you like it," he said, handing me the present. "Sorry about the wrapping paper, that's all I could find at my house."

"It's perfect." It was wrapped in comics from the newspaper. It was obvious he had done it himself. I couldn't have been happier, even if he'd showed up with a present that looked like Martha Stewart had wrapped it.

Like James, I tore open the present. It was a book on star constellations. "Thank you. I love it," I exclaimed. The book made me feel closer to him.

"That's not the whole present," he said, laughing.

"It's not?"

I watched as James opened the black case. Inside was a telescope for stargazing. "This is mine. I brought it over to show you the real stars that are outlined in the book." He assembled it swiftly and then took my hand. "Come on. Let's set it up where there won't be any trees in the way. It's such a clear night, it should be perfect." We walked over to a clear spot by the green house. In no time, he set it up. "I remembered that you said the stars on your ceiling kept the nightmares away, so I thought maybe if you saw the real ones up close they might comfort you at night too. I hope you don't think it's a corny present," he added in a whisper.

"Of course not." I wrapped my arms around him, reached up on my tiptoes, and kissed him so that he'd know how much it meant to me. "It's the best present ever." I kissed him again, deeper this time. I ran my hands through his soft hair while he held me close. Our tongues teased each other, darting in and out of each other's mouths. We pulled away, breathing heavily.

Leaning his forehead against mine, he said, "I'm glad you like it."

"Show me how it works." I was still trying to slow down my racing heart.

"Absolutely. I know I already showed you the Big Dipper and the Little Dipper," he explained, his voice filled with the same passion as when he talked about football. "I wanted to show you how cool they look when you see them through the telescope." He pointed it at the sky and adjusted several dials. "Here, take a look," he whispered.

"Amazing. The night sky is beautiful." I'd never looked through a telescope. Now I understood why James found this so comforting and calming. I'd have to look out my window the next time a nightmare woke me up. I was sure it would help. I felt closer to James then ever. He was sharing a piece of himself with me.

We spent the next half hour looking through the telescope at the different constellations. He showed me how to use the telescope and I even located the Little Dipper on my own. "I found it. The Little Dipper," I said with excitement. "Take a look." I made room for him.

"Good job. You're a quick learner."

"You're a good teacher."

He smiled.

"I'm sure I'll sleep better now, knowing that these stars are right outside my window. This was such a thoughtful gift."

"I'm so glad you like it."

"I love it. Hey, you never told me why you have trouble sleeping?"

"That's a story for another day," he answered, avoiding my question. His posture had become stiff. "Today's all about you. It's your birthday."

"Exactly. Please tell me," I placed my hand on the side of his face. "I want to know."

Slowly he nodded. "Sometimes I can't sleep because my house is too noisy." He took a deep breath before continuing. "My mom and dad argue a lot. My room is next to theirs and I can't sleep when they're shouting. It can get really ugly." *Does his dad hit his mom? Is that what Tyler's comment meant the other night?*

"I'm here, if you ever want to talk about it."

"Thanks, that means a lot to me." He took my face in his hands and pressed his lips against mine. I felt his invisible wall all but disappear.

"I love you," I whispered, in between kisses.

"What?" he asked, surprised. Tonight was the first time I'd told him. It had been true for weeks, but I hadn't had the courage to say it out loud. "Say it again." He smiled.

"I love you, James Muldoon," I repeated loud and clear, wanting to shout it to the world.

"I love you too," he whispered, pulling me even closer to him. The rest of the world ceased to exist when I was with James. He began kissing my lips until they felt bruised and swollen. Then he trailed kisses down my neck to the sensitive spot behind my ear. I felt him hard against my leg and I moaned as I pressed against him, wanting more.

"This isn't right," he said, pulling away. He took a step back, running his hands through his hair. He looked like he was struggling to get his hormones under control.

I moved toward him, gently placing my hand on his arm. "I love you James. I want to be with you." I thought about the wish I'd made earlier when I blew out my candles.

He took both of my hands in his and placed them over his heart. "You don't know how happy it makes me feel to hear you say that. But I can't make love to you right now."

"Why not?" I asked, choking up. Tears welled in my eyes.

"Please don't cry." He gently wiped a tear away with his fingertips. "It's not what you think. I want to be with you, more than anything." There was pain in his handsome face as he explained, "You scared the crap out of me when you collapsed at school. You just spent two days in the hospital having an emergency appendectomy. I won't do anything that might cause you pain. I can't. I love you too much. If anything happened to you, I'd never forgive myself."

"I'm sorry. You're right," I readily agreed, feeling bad for upsetting him. "The doctor did say to take it easy for a couple of weeks."

"I promise you, Mikayla, I want to make love to you. My strength is tested every time we're together, but I want to do the right thing."

"What if I promise to behave until I'm healed?" He looked so distraught I would have suggested just about anything if thought it'd help.

He chuckled. "Thanks. That would make things a little easier."

"Okay," I replied, hoping I'd be able to follow through.

"It's getting late. I should pack up my telescope and head home. I told your mom that I wouldn't keep you up late. She wants you to get enough rest."

He walked me to the front door. "I had a perfect birthday. Thank you. And to answer your question from earlier this afternoon, I am very happy."

"I'm glad." He smiled and his eyes were a fathomless deep green. Green was becoming my favorite color. He kissed me one more time, "Happy birthday."

"Goodnight, James."

"Goodnight," he called, walking out to his truck, but waiting until I went inside before leaving.

Minutes later I crawled under my covers. It had been a long day. Before closing my eyes, I looked up at the ceiling. Thousands of little stars were shining. James had done this. It was another birthday present. I scanned the ceiling for the constellations that he had taught me. I found the Little Dipper and smiled, feeling safe. I hadn't known that it was possible to love him more than I already did.

Chapter Twenty

Dooner

The following two and a half weeks sped by. Every day I hurried home to eat dinner and then headed over to Mikayla's. We'd sit on her porch, swim in our private swimming hole, or go for a ride in Old Faithful. One Saturday night we even went to see one of my favorite country singers, Kenny Chesney. Mikayla looked so damn hot that night it almost blew my mind. I smiled as I pictured her moving to the music in her short jean skirt, cowboy hat, and cowboy boots. We hadn't had sex yet, but every time we were together it got harder and harder to hold ourselves back. Suddenly I realized I needed to get my thoughts under control and think about something else. I was standing in the middle of the guys' locker room and I wouldn't want one of the guys to look over here, see my erection, and get the wrong idea.

Coach opened the door and yelled, "Dooner, Tyler, and Casey, get your asses in here as soon as you're decent." Did this mean he had good news to tell us? We'd been working our butts off ever since he put us on suspension, following through with our plan to get the team in shape to play a passing game instead of a running game. Additionally, the animosity between us, both on and off the field, had disappeared. I was sure Coach had noticed. Hopefully he was going to lift the ban. The big opening game was only three days away.

We got ready in record time. Nervously, I knocked on Coach's door.

"Come on in," he said. We stepped hesitantly into his office. We all had a lot riding on this game.

He motioned for us to sit down in the chairs facing his desk. I held my breath as Coach leaned back in his chair. "I'm going to give it to you guys straight up. I'm not happy about the fight that took place at the beginning of the season on my field." He paused for effect. "However, I'd have to be blind not to notice the change in you three. You've worked hard during practice and during your secret sessions...yes, I know about those." He nodded his head. "I can't believe I'm going to do this, but your team's been pressuring me to let you all play in the opening game. You've earned their respect by being real team captains. You've taught them new plays to capitalize on their strengths. I'm proud of you. Your teammates want the three of you out on that field with them on Friday night, so I'm going to grant them their wish. Don't make me regret it."

Finally I let out my breath. Those were the words I'd been waiting to hear for weeks. I wanted to scream and do a victory dance, I was so happy.

"Thank you, Coach," we said simultaneously.

"Go, get on outta here and tell the team." He waved us out. "Dooner, hold up a second, I need to talk to you." I wondered what this was about? I watched Tyler and Casey leave, closing the door behind them. Hesitantly, I sat back down on the edge of the chair. I heard the rest of the team celebrating in the locker room. Tyler and Casey must have told them the good news.

"What is it, Coach?" I asked, trying not to sound as nervous as I felt.

"I wanted you to know that I received a phone call last

week. It was from the coach at Texas Tech. He said it looks like your application is all in order and he wants to come and watch you play as soon as possible. He may even be at the game this Friday. I need to know if this school is still your first choice or if you've changed your mind."

"Texas Tech is still my first choice. I'd love nothing more than to play for them."

"Okay, that's what I needed to know." He nodded his head in approval. "It looks like you'll do fine out there this season. You're more than ready. If all goes well, we'll set you up with an official visit to Texas Tech."

"Thanks, Coach, for everything." I wanted to say more, but words got caught in my throat. I knew he would understand what I meant. He had always been more than just a coach to me.

"Good luck, son," he said as he opened the door.

The locker room had cleared out by the time my conversation with Coach was over. I walked with an extra swagger in my step out to my truck. I couldn't imagine how this day could get any better. I couldn't wait to tell Mikayla the good news. I thought about driving straight over to her house, but my stomach growled. I'd tell her as soon as I'd eaten lunch.

When I got home my mom was at the kitchen table, writing out a grocery list. "Hey, Mom. Where's Dad? I didn't see his truck in the driveway." I hung up my keys by the back door. I walked over to the refrigerator and grabbed a yellow Gatorade.

"I think he went to the Moose Lodge. Today's two for Tuesday and free pizza."

"Makes sense," I replied. My dad always ended up wherever there was a drink special.

"Did you need something?" she asked, sounding concerned.

It was rare that I asked about his whereabouts. "No, I was

just curious." The whole way home I thought about what his reaction would be when I told him I'd be playing in the game on Friday. I knew he'd be happy, but he'd find fault somewhere, ruining my good mood. He always had to bitch about something. He was never completely happy unless he was putting someone down. I was glad I could hold off until later to tell him. Also I'd wanted Mikayla to be the first one I told.

I sat down to eat the two sandwiches that my mom put in front of me. Nothing tasted better than a turkey sandwich with tomato after a grueling practice. I had almost finished one sandwich when there was a light knock at the back door. I jumped. Who could that be? No one ever came to visit. My mom looked just as surprised. "I'll get it," I said, pushing back from the table.

Mikayla stood at the door. *"What's she doing here?"* I screamed inside my head. Her mom's car was parked in the driveway, and it looked as out of place as she did. I thought that she understood that there was a good reason why I'd never invited her over. I began to panic, sweat beading on my forehead.

She stared at me, confused by my stunned silence. "Well, James, are you going to invite me in or are you just going to stand there?" Mikayla asked, her hands on her hips. I knew if I didn't answer her soon, she was going to run. Maybe she should.

"Who is it?" said my mom, coming to see. When she saw Mikayla standing on our doorstep, she quickly gushed, "Come on in, sweetie." She pushed past me and opened the door, "I'm sorry my son doesn't have any manners." She glared harshly at me. "I'm not sure what has gotten into him. I'm Mrs. Muldoon, Jimmy's mom. And you must be his girlfriend, Mikayla. I've heard so much about you." *What? I never talk about my personal life.*

"Hi, I'm Mike," she said, extending her hand out to my

mom. My mom clasped it tightly.

I stood by, dumbfounded. I hadn't said so much as hello. I was having a hard time believing any of this was real.

My mom led Mikayla to an empty chair at the kitchen table. Robotically, I sat back down in front of my half-eaten lunch. Suddenly, I'd lost my appetite. I stared at my plate.

"Have you eaten lunch? I'd be happy to make you something to eat," my mom offered.

"No thank you, I just ate." I could feel Mikayla's eyes boring into me, but I didn't look up. I was trying to figure out what to do. Should I pretend that it was okay for her to stop by? Or should I make up an excuse to get her out of here? My dad was probably going to be gone for awhile, but what if he came back early?

My mom seemed oblivious of the tension in the room. She babbled, "How about a cookie then? I just made them this morning. They're Jimmy's favorite, cowboy cookies."

"Thanks, I'd love one." Mikayla took one from the platter my mom set down on the table. "Umm...these are delicious," she exclaimed, taking a bite.

"Thank you." Picking her grocery list off the table, she said. "Well, I'd love to stay and get to know you better, but I was just leaving to go to the store. Jimmy here," she said, patting me on the back, "eats me out of house and home." She smiled. "It was nice meeting you. Now I understand why he's in such a hurry to finish his dinner every night."

"Mom," I snarled, lifting my eyes from my plate. I glanced at Mikayla, but she wasn't looking at me.

"It was nice to meet you too, Mrs. Muldoon." She smiled warmly.

"Come back again real soon, okay?"

"Okay."

"Have fun, kids. I'll be back in a couple of hours." My mom grabbed her purse and left.

Mikayla stood. "I'm leaving too. It's obvious coming here

was a big mistake."

"Why'd you come?" I asked angrily, finally speaking.

"I had something exciting to tell you and I didn't want to wait. I wanted you to be the first to know." It looked like she was about to burst into tears. Instantly I felt like a jackass for upsetting her.

She had her hand on the handle of the back door when I reached her. I spun her around, "I'm sorry for being a jerk. It's no excuse, but you caught me off guard. I don't want you to go." I took a deep breath. I knew if I wanted her to stay I'd have to be completely honest with her. "You're the first friend to come over. Ever."

"Really?" she asked, a surprised look on her face.

"Really. And I don't just mean that you're the first girlfriend I've had over. You're the first friend of any kind to come over."

"Why?"

"It's complicated." She had her hand on the handle again. I knew if I didn't tell her the whole truth I'd lose her for good. Quickly I said, "I've been too embarrassed to ask anyone over, including you. My parents fight a lot and I never know when they're going to go at it. It can get pretty ugly. There are even holes in the wall to prove how bad it gets sometimes." I looked into her eyes and she wasn't pitying or judging me. Her deep brown eyes were understanding. "But I'm asking you now-please stay."

"Okay." She nodded. It felt good to confide in her. I should have been more honest weeks ago. I loved her and she loved me. I should have known she could've handled the truth. She was tough. There was more to tell, and I was ready to tell her everything, but right now I wanted to hear about her good news and share mine with her.

"Come on back in the kitchen. I want to hear your good news." I held her hand as we walked back to the table. We sat down again and this time I looked into her beautiful brown eyes. They were filled with excitement. "So, what is it?"

"It's only the best news ever! Months ago I submitted a painting to be part of a highly recognized teen art exhibit in New York City, and they chose mine out of thousands of entries. Also, they want my painting to be on the cover of the brochure and on some of the posters advertising the exhibit! Isn't that amazing?"

"I always knew you talented. I'm so happy for you." I squeezed her hand.

"This will help me get into Boston University to study fine art."

"That's great," I said, with just a hint of sadness. Thankfully Mikayla was too excited to notice. The truth was I'd been so wrapped up in my own dream of going to Texas Tech that I hadn't even thought about the fact that Mikayla might be going to a college thousands of miles away from me. It was going to hurt to be that far from her, but we'd worry about that later. Right now it was time to focus on the positives.

"The exhibit runs from October until February. There's an opening awards ceremony that I've been invited to attend. I want to know if you could come with me? It would mean a lot to me if you were there."

"Of course I'll be by your side. I wouldn't miss it for the world. I'm honored that you want me there." I placed my free hand over my heart.

"Thanks." She jumped up and hugged me.

I pushed my chair back and pulled her onto my lap. She giggled. "I got good news too today. Coach is letting me play in the opening game." I smiled broadly. "And there might even be a scout there to watch me play."

"That's great. You've been practicing hard all summer. I'm sure the scouts will recognize your talent. Pops says you're the best football player this town's ever seen." Whispering, she added, "He even said you could go pro someday."

"Your pops said that, really?" Having him say that meant

a lot to me. I respected his opinion.

"Yes, he did." She laughed. "I'll have to come and watch you play. I've never been to a football game before."

"I'll have to make sure I play my very best then. It'll be great knowing that you're in the stands, cheering me on."

"It's pretty cool that we both got great news today. We should do something special to celebrate." She smiled devilishly, making me wonder what she was planning, although I had a pretty good idea. I wasn't all that surprised when she said, "Why don't you give me a tour?"

My mom and dad would both be gone for a while, so I figured what the hell. Nothing could ruin this perfect day. "Sure, I'll show you around. But I'm warning you, there isn't much to see."

I quickly led her through the downstairs, which was small. It consisted of only three rooms, the kitchen, the dining room, and the living room. Except for the football trophies crowding the mantle, these rooms had little to do with me. I spent all my time in my room when I was home. I continued to hold her hand as we climbed the stairs to the second floor.

"This is my room," I said, pulling her inside and closing the door behind us. I watched her as she looked around, trying to see what my room must look like through her eyes. There were several posters of the solar system hanging on the walls that I'd gotten as birthday presents when I was a kid, but other than that, it was pretty plain. I didn't even have any dirty clothes on the floor.

"So what do you think of my room? Not what you expected, I bet." I smiled nervously. I couldn't believe Mikayla was actually in my bedroom.

"It's neat, just like I thought it would be." She paused, picking up a book on my desk, reading the title, and then putting it back down. "I'm surprised, though, that you don't have more stuff around. Why's that?"

Since I was being honest, I said, "For as long as I can

remember, I've been counting down the days until I got outta here. I figured the less stuff I had to move, the better. Of course, that changed when I met you. You've given me a reason to want to stay." I grabbed her hand and walked her over to the nightstand next to my bed where I'd placed the portrait of her that she'd drawn. "See, I have the one thing that matters."

"Me too," she said, leaning in close. She smelled so good.

"You've become the most important thing in my life." I brought her hand to my lips and kissed it. Slowly I kissed each fingertip. "I hope that doesn't scare you."

"No, it doesn't scare me. How I feel right now scares me." She trembled slightly.

Together we fell back onto the bed. This was the right moment. Mikayla had seen a part of me that no one else ever had. And she loved me anyway. Here she was in my room and in my bed. I'd already shared almost all of my secrets with her. Now I wanted to share this with her too. I took a deep breath, wanting to take things slow. It was important to me that Mikayla enjoyed making love to me as much as I was going to enjoy making love to her.

I kissed her lips until they were bruised and swollen. Then I moved my mouth down her neck to the sensitive spot behind her ear until her breathing came in raspy gasps. Once again I had to remind myself to slow down. Her hands tangled in my hair.

I pulled away to catch my breath. "Are you sure you want to do this?"

"Yes. I want you to make love to me."

There was no more need for words. I quickly stripped off my clothes and tossed them on the floor. Mikayla did the same. She was so beautiful. I couldn't take my eyes off of her. I simply stared at her perfect body, trying to imprint it on my memory. I didn't ever want to forget this moment. Swiftly I repositioned us, so that she was underneath me. I lowered my head to her breast and pulled her nipple into my mouth. She tasted sweet. Taking my time, I trailed kisses down to her navel.

We were both ready for this next step in our relationship. We went slowly, exploring each other's bodies, savoring every touch. My body responded to her soft caresses. Gently I parted her legs and touched her. She sighed with pleasure. Soon we were both on the brink of ecstasy. Knowing we couldn't hang on much longer, I ripped open a condom. I positioned myself between her legs and gently entered her. She gasped.

"Did I hurt you?" I asked worriedly.

"No." She grabbed my hips and pulling me toward her. "It feels wonderful."

I knew what she meant. Nothing could compare to how great this felt. I bit my lip to stop myself from feeling too much all at once. I moved slowly at first and then, when her breathing came faster, I thrust harder.

Trembling, she called out, "I love you, James."

Then it was my turn. Everything I felt for her came pouring out at once. Spent, I collapsed on the bed and pulled her into my arms. "I love you, Mikayla."

We stayed curled up together in my bed for as long as I dared. "We should probably get dressed. It's getting late." I feared what would happen if my dad came back early.

We found our clothes and quickly got dressed. Once we were back downstairs I asked, "Do you want something to eat? I'm hungry."

"Wow," Mikayla said, looking at the clock in the kitchen. "I can't believe it's three o'clock already. I promised I'd have my mom's car back by now. She had errands to run. I better go." She made her way to the backdoor, and I followed her.

"Okay, I'll see you tomorrow morning," I said. I didn't want her to go, but I knew it was time.

"Oh, yeah. I almost forgot tomorrow's the first day of school."

"Do you want me to pick you up?" I couldn't wait to see her again.

"No, that's okay. I'll catch a ride with my mom. She's going in the same direction, and it's her first day too. I'll wait for you in the parking lot though." She smiled brightly.

"Perfect." I walked with her out to her mom's car. "I'm glad you stopped by today." I leaned down and kissed her soft lips one last time. I still couldn't believe what we'd shared today. I hadn't known it was possible to love someone so much.

She was backing out of the driveway when I saw my dad's truck coming down the road. He accelerated, no doubt trying to figure out who was leaving. I waited in the driveway to tell him my good news about Friday's game.

His tires screeched to a halt and he quickly jumped out of his truck, slamming the door. His face was red and he smelled like cheap whiskey and cigarettes. He looked mad. "Who the fuck was that?" He nodded down the road in the direction that Mikayla had gone. "I know that fancy car isn't from around here. I think I've seen it parked in the driveway at Mr. Jenkins' place. I heard his rich daughter, Sarah, moved back here. She has a couple of teenage daughters, doesn't she? Don't answer that. It's written all over your face." He laughed darkly. "You should've taken my warning seriously. A girl like that's nothing but trouble."

"What warning?"

"I told you weeks ago that girls are trouble. Your only focus should be football and winning that scholarship. And yet, you ignored me, and invited that whore to my house. What were you two doing, fucking on my couch?"

"Mikayla is not some whore." I felt my own temper rising. Then a calm came over me as I realized I no longer cared what my dad thought. I had everything I needed. "You're a pathetic drunk," I stated, shrugging. I turned to leave. I took half a step when I was yanked roughly back by my shirt. I spun around and faced him.

"Just where do you think you're going, Jimmy?"

"I don't know yet, but anywhere's better than here."

"You're not going anywhere." My dad shook his head.

"You can't stop me." I was bigger than my dad and I had been for a while now.

"Sure I can." My dad lifted his hand and punched me hard in the gut.

I didn't flinch. I'd anticipated he'd try something like that. It wasn't the first time my dad had used force. Only difference was I wasn't ten years old anymore. I suspected it hurt him more than it had hurt me. He rubbed his knuckles. "Let's see what you got, boy," he taunted.

"I'm not going to fight you," I said. I refused to be like him.

"You're a pussy," he slurred.

"No. You're just not worth it."

His eyes took on a dangerous look. His face was contorted with rage, but he remained eerily calm. He didn't make another move to strike at me. His voice was steady when he spoke. "You might have won this round, Jimmy. But this is far from over." I took a step toward where I'd parked Old Faithful. My dad called out, "That city girl ain't your type. Look around, boy, you're not good enough for a girl like that, she's from a completely different world. If I ever see her poking her nose around here again, you'll both be sorry." Then he walked away, probably to pour himself another drink.

I didn't like how calm my dad had been. I also didn't like the fact that he'd threatened Mikayla. He knew he couldn't physically harm me, so he figured he'd hurt me the only way he could. By hurting Mikayla. I had a sick feeling in the pit of my stomach. I climbed into Old Faithful and headed down the road. My first impulse was to drive over to Mikayla's and tell the rest of my secrets- how my dad was a violent man, hitting my mom, and even us kids when we were younger. I thought about warning Mikayla. I wouldn't put it past my dad to carry out his threat and hurt her if the opportunity ever presented itself. In the end, I drove on by. I couldn't risk involving her. I'd do anything to protect her, even if it broke my own heart.

Chapter Twenty-One

Mike

I tried on the raspberry colored T-shirt that Emma gave me for my birthday. It was the third shirt I'd tried on this morning. Normally, I put on the first clothes I grabbed, but today I wanted to look perfect when I saw James. I looked in the mirror one last time, feeling mostly satisfied with my reflection. My hair curled in every direction, but that couldn't be helped.

I rushed down the stairs and joined Emma at the kitchen table to eat a quick breakfast. "Okay, let's go," my mom said nervously a few minutes later.

Pops shuffled into the kitchen. "I want to wish you all good luck on your first day. Not that you need it." He grinned.

Impulsively, I hugged him. I was going to miss helping him with his crossword puzzles and listening to his clichés.

"You are coming back, aren't you?" he joked when I pulled away.

"Of course." I laughed. "Just don't miss us too much."

"Please." He waved his hand in the air. "I was taking care of myself a long time before you all showed up on my doorstep."

"Bye Pops." I smiled, knowing he'd changed since we moved in, even if he didn't like to admit it. He seemed happier and younger.

My mom and Emma waved goodbye to him.

"Are you girls ready for your first day at Railroad Mills High? Are you nervous?" my mom asked once we were settled into her car.

Emma leaned forward and answered without pause, "I'm not one bit nervous. It's such a small town, I feel like I already know everybody. I'm meeting the other cheerleaders in the parking lot so we can make a grand entrance." I grinned. That was Emma, always wanting to be the center of attention.

"I'm happy for you," my mom nodded. "And Mike, what about you? Are you still upset about beginning your senior year at a new school?"

I looked over at my mom and grinned. "I'm happy we moved here." I was no longer the angry girl who was forced to move three thousand miles away from all of her friends. Nowhere had changed me. I reached out and lightly touched my mom's arm, "You were right, Mom, this is the right place for us, after all," I said, repeating my mom's words from the day we arrived. "What about you? Are you ready for your big debut?"

"Yes, yes I am." She smiled contently.

As we pulled into the parking lot, I took in the sight of all the trucks. We definitely weren't in California anymore, where the school parking lot had been filled with brand new shiny Mercedes and BMWs. Here there were Chevy and Ford pick-up trucks of all sizes and colors. As I scanned the lot, it appeared as if everyone matched their truck the way some dog owners looked like their dogs. For example, Tyler's girlfriend, Liz, a perky bleached blonde cheerleader, owned a small, bright blue Jeep Liberty. Tank, who had to be the biggest guy at school, drove a gigantic Ford pick-up truck the kind used for plowing snow. And a kid with spiked hair wearing dark clothes and a dog collar leaned against a rusted black truck covered in graffiti. However, it only took only a second to realize that the one pick-up that mattered to me most wasn't here yet.

Emma had spotted her friends and was the first to get out of the car. "Bye Mom, Mike," Emma called over her shoulder, walking off to join them. They jumped around and laughed excitedly. Emma fit right in with these girls; it was like she'd lived here her whole life.

I climbed out next. "I'm going to wait here. James and I made plans to meet in the parking lot." I shut my door and walked around to the back and stood leaning against the car. "Go on in," I said, waving my hand at my mom. "I'm sure he'll be here any minute." She looked anxious to get to her classroom.

"Oh, okay. I guess I should go in and make sure everything's in order." She reached into the backseat and grabbed her bag. "Are you sure you'll be alright?"

"Yeah, I'm sure." I nodded.

"Okay, but don't be late."

"Please, mom." I rolled my eyes.

I watched as she entered the school. She was wearing a tan-colored skirt and a short-sleeved white blouse, her wavy hair pulled back into a giant clip. Mostly I noticed the big smile she wore on her face. She looked the happiest she had in a long time. She was going to be an awesome teacher. I wished my dad could've seen her now; he would've been so proud.

I checked the time. Only five more minutes until the bell rang. What could be keeping James? I wondered if it had anything to do with what happened between us yesterday. As quickly as that thought occurred to me, I dismissed it. Yesterday was the best day of my life and I knew that it was for him too. I sighed. I called him, but it went directly to voice mail.

When he hadn't shown up by the time the five minutes were up, I joined the crowd of students and entered the building. I'd come in over the summer a couple of times to help my mom, so I knew my way around, finding my locker without any difficulty. My locker number and combination had come in the mail last week, along with my class schedule. I dialed the combination and it opened on the first try. The locker assignments were in alphabetical order, which meant that James' was next to mine. He still hadn't arrived by the time I'd stowed my meager belongings. I slammed my locker shut and headed towards my first block class. I had advanced drawing and the art room was on the opposite side of the school down by the cafeteria.

The class seemed to drag by. Finally it was over and I rushed out, hurrying back upstairs to the senior hallway. I wanted to find James before my next class started. Only I didn't see him anywhere. *How hard can it be to find a guy who's 6 foot 4 inches tall?* I saw a group of kids in T-shirts and jeans hanging out by the top of the staircase, catching up on summer gossip and giving each other high fives, but James wasn't among them. I was starting to worry that something was wrong.

"Hi Mike. How's your first day so far?" Tyler asked, breaking away from his friends when he saw me.

"Good. Hey, have you seen James this morning?"

He paused, scratching his head. "Now that you mention it, no I haven't. The teacher called his name during my last class, but he wasn't there. We all just assumed that there was a change with the class list. I'm sure he's here. We have our big game coming up in two more days. Did you hear? Coach lifted our suspension. Dooner and I are both starting on Friday."

"I did hear. Congratulations."

"What class do you have now?" Tyler asked.

"Economics."

"Me too," he answered. I was relieved that he did most of the talking, complaining that the teacher from his last class assigned homework on the first day.

As we entered Economics, the teacher announced, "Come in and sit down. It doesn't matter where, because I have a seating chart. Alphabetical order." He waved a paper around in the air for everyone to see while grumbles erupted. It didn't matter to me where I sat, because James wasn't in this class. I wouldn't be seeing him until next period.

The teacher didn't waste time. "Welcome to Economics. For those of you who don't know me, I'm Mr. John. When I call your name, please move to the seat I assign you."

I tuned out as he called out the names until I heard my own. He pointed to an empty desk in the back row. *Ugh!* I thought as I sat down next to Casey, having no choice in the matter.

"Hi Mike." Casey grinned. "How are you feeling? I haven't seen you since you walked into the boys' locker room. I heard you ended up in the hospital that day."

"Yeah, I had my appendix removed." I didn't elaborate. I still didn't trust this guy.

"Really? Wow, you look great." I felt his eyes roam over me. I shivered in disgust. Casey didn't seem to notice my discomfort. "As a matter of fact, you're even hotter than I remembered. You have great legs. You should be on the cheerleading squad." He nodded his head in approval.

"No, thanks. I leave that to Emma. Aren't the two of you an item?" I reminded him, wanting to switch his focus from me to her.

"Well, yeah, but, there's enough of me to go around."

"You're gross." I gave Casey a piercing look and turned around to face the teacher who'd finished assigning seats and was ready to begin.

Once again class dragged by. Each minute felt like an hour. The only thing that got me through was the fact that James was in my next class. When it was finally over, I gathered my things and left quickly, ignoring Casey when he called after me. Still no sign of James at his locker. I headed to

English with the bell ringing. Panicking, I decided if he didn't show up by lunch, I was going to ditch school to find him. Something was wrong.

There were only two empty seats left by the time I got to class. I chose the one in the back, next to a girl I recognized from my art class. She smiled as I took my seat.

I saw Casey sitting two rows over. He winked at me and grabbed his crotch. He was the most foul human being I'd ever met. I sure hope Emma knew what she was doing with this creep.

Seconds later, I was flooded with relief when James walked in. He took the last empty seat in the front row, on the opposite side of the room from where I was sitting. *Oh well, we'll be sitting next to each other as soon as the teacher pulls out the alphabetical seating chart.*

"Good morning class," the teacher said, clearing her throat. "I'm Mrs. Allen. Welcome to your senior year of English. I believe that you are now old enough to choose your own seats. I assume that when you came into the room that you sat down next to one of your friends. You may keep that seat, unless of course you can't handle that, at which point I'll find a new one for you. Everyone understand?"

The room filled with cries of joy. Everyone was happy, but me. *Really?* I wanted to scream out loud. So far I was off to a terrible start at Railroad Mills High. First James hadn't been in the parking lot like we planned. Then I got hit on all last period by Casey the perv, and now this. James had finally showed up and he hadn't even acknowledged me, like he'd forgotten that I existed.

Mrs. Allen continued to talk, "We'll be busy in here this year. We will complete assignments as a whole group, with partners, and independently. The first assignment is a partner activity. You will interview the person sitting next to you and then report back to the class. It's an opportunity to get to know each other better while working on effective communication skills. Take a copy of the questionnaire and then pass the rest back. Get started as soon as you have one."

I watched as James focused all his attention on the bubbly brunette wearing lots of eyeliner sitting next to him. I glared angrily at them, thinking about my next move, until the girl next to me tapped me on the arm.

"Mike, is it? I'm Gina Jo." She stuck her hand out and I shook it. "Do you want to be my partner for this assignment?"

"Sure. That would be great," I responded, trying to forget about James for the moment. I would have to wait until class was over to ask him what was going on.

"They're both jerks." She nodded her head at James and the brunette. "Marilyn is one of the biggest sluts in the school. I've heard that she's slept with every guy on the football team." My eyes opened wide, encouraging her to go on. "And Dooner, he's more an enigma. But he is among the popular crowd." She said it like it was a bad thing.

I didn't tell her that he was supposed to be my boyfriend. Instead I carefully probed her for information. "What do you mean he's an enigma?"

"He's cute, he's smart, but for the most part he keeps to himself. He thinks he's better than everyone else." She rolled her eyes. "Girls are always hanging on his every word. As far as I know though, he's never had a girlfriend." This made me smile until she added, "Liz, the cheerleading captain, is always trying to sink her claws into him." She leaned in closer and whispered, "I heard that they even hooked up once."

I couldn't keep the surprise out of my voice as I said, "You mean Liz, as in Tyler's girlfriend?" I just couldn't picture it.

"Oh, yeah, I'm sorry. I forgot he's your cousin." She turned red. "I didn't mean to be spreading rumors."

"That's okay. Don't worry about it." I waved it off like it was no big deal. "When did Tyler and Liz start going out? I can't remember what he told me."

She shrugged. "Over the summer, I think. I didn't even

know they were a couple until I saw them making out at the lockers this morning."

I had to wait until class was over to talk to James. When the bell rang, I was surprised to see him waiting for me at the door. Maybe I was overreacting to Gina Jo's comments and the fact that I hadn't spoken to him yet. He looked so handsome, standing there with his hair tousled and his book tucked casually under his arm. I let out a sigh. He deserved to be able to explain himself before I jumped to conclusions. A smile spread across my face. I must not let my imagination get so carried away next time.

"Hi Mikayla," James said quietly. His eyes were a cloudy greenish grey. *Something is wrong.*

"Hi," I said nervously. Nothing about this felt right. I was scared to think what it could be.

Leading me down the hall, he said, "We need to talk." His face was hard. There was no trace of the boy I'd proclaimed my love to only twenty-four hours ago. I barely recognized the person standing next to me. "Let's go somewhere more private." There was a lot of noise in the hall. Everyone was getting ready to go to lunch.

"No, whatever you have to say to me, you can say it here." I knew if we left the crowded hall it would be worse. I knew I wasn't going to like what he had to say.

He looked around. "Okay, if that's what you want." He took a deep breath. "This isn't going to work, you and me. I don't want to see you anymore."

I knew it was going to be bad, but this was completely unexpected. "What?" I managed to get out. It was all I could do to keep from bursting into tears. I bit my lip.

"I don't want to be with you," he repeated a second time.

A full minute passed before I could respond. My throat was tight. My stomach hurt. I felt like someone had punched me in the gut. The hall was mostly empty now. "That's what I thought you said, only I don't believe it. I don't understand.

Did I do something wrong?"

"I..." he stuttered. He looked away and then back again at me again. His eyes were cold and distant. Out of the corner of my eye I saw Liz pass nearby. I watched as James followed her with his eyes. "I'm in love with somebody else. I met someone long before you rolled into town and I thought it was over, but it's not. Being with you made me realize I love her and not you. Yesterday meant nothing to me. Nothing."

His face was serious, but his voice cracked, making me question whether or not he was telling the truth. I knew what passed between us when we were making love, and trust me it wasn't nothing. Staring at James, I sensed that something else was going on underneath this hard façade. His walls were back up, and I smelled fear. *What is he scared of?*

"You don't mean that." I reached out to touch him, trying to break through. He stepped back. *Wow, that really hurts.*

"Don't," he said harshly. Turning, he walked away without another saying another word.

I stood frozen in the middle of the hallway, concentrating on breathing in and out. James didn't look back. He walked down the hall and then disappeared around the corner. He'd ripped my heart out and he didn't even seem to care.

The rest of the day passed in a blur. I was too numb to pay attention to anything my teachers said. I wasn't even sure how I made it from class to class. I was angry at myself for believing I was actually happy here in Nowhere. How could I have I been so stupid?

After school I rode home with my mom, listening to her babble about her classes and her students. She was so happy that she didn't even notice that I barely said two words the whole way home. Walking through the door, I made an excuse about having to do homework, and raced up the steps to my room. I even avoided Pops, fearing that he'd be able to see through me and know that something was wrong. I didn't want to talk about it just yet. I needed time.

Once in my room, I finally let out the tears that had threatened to spill all afternoon. Crying helped a little, but I was still hurt and angry. Sighing, I reached for my sketchpad and pencils. For the next hour, my hand flew across the page, making dark lines with my charcoal pencil.

Suddenly Emma came bursting into the room, startling me. My pencil gouged the paper. "Damn it, Emma."

"Sorry." She shrugged. She began throwing clothes around while she went on and on about how wonderful her day had been. I didn't listen to anything she said.

"Are you done? I'm busy," I snapped, irritated.

She stopped what she was doing. Looking at me for the first time since she came barging into the room, she said, "What's the matter with you? You're not feeling sick again, are you?" Ever since I had my appendix out, things between us had changed. Emma and I had been getting along.

"No, I'm not sick again." She looked relieved.

"What's wrong then?"

I figured it was best to just get it out. Emma would hear all about it from her gossipy cheerleading friends anyway. I took a deep breath. "James dumped me today." My voice cracked and I began to cry again.

"No way." She sat down next to me on the bed. Acting like a true sister, she hugged me and let me cry on her shoulder. Once I'd calmed, she asked, "What happened? You two always seemed so happy together."

"He said that he's in love with someone else." It hurt to say that out loud. I felt like I might throw up.

"Really?" Emma's face registered surprise at first. Then, after a long pause, she looked almost guilty.

"What is it?" I demanded. "What did you do?"

"I didn't do anything."

"Tell me," I demanded. Emma knew more than she was saying.

Taking her time to respond, she sputtered, "Well,

remember the Saturday night that you were home sick, right before you got your appendix out?"

"Yeah..." I answered, not understanding where she was going with this.

"I don't know how to say this." I glared at her in impatience. She continued in a rush. "I was hanging out, drinking with some of the girls, and we ended up at the school looking for something to do. Suddenly we noticed Liz was gone and we went to look for her. Sometimes her and Tyler sneak off in a dark corner of the gym to hook up. We decided to go and spy on her. Only she wasn't in the make-out corner with Tyler, like we'd thought." She looked and me and winced. I nodded at her to continue. I already knew what she was going to say. "She was with Dooner." I didn't cry. I was all cried out. "They were kissing."

"Why didn't you tell me?" I moved away from her.

"I'm sorry. I was going to tell you, but then you got sick. When you came home from the hospital, I saw your face light up when you saw him sitting on the porch. I told myself that I'd imagined the whole thing. You both seemed so in love with each other, spending all of your free time together. Even made me jealous."

"Wow," I replied, once I found my voice. "I thought maybe he'd been lying to me, but I guess he wasn't."

Chapter Twenty-Two

Dooner

I was the first one to arrive in the locker room for the big game. I needed a moment alone to collect myself before the rest of the team arrived. My whole future was riding on this game. I sat down on the bench and put my elbows on my knees. I focused on breathing. I'd been a mess for the past two days. Ever since I broke up with Mikayla. I closed my eyes, remembering how my heart shattered when I saw what my words did to her. I still couldn't believe how easily she accepted my lies. Of course I wasn't in love with anyone else. I made it all up to protect her. I loved her so much I'd let her go.

It had been hard seeing her at school from a distance, when I all I really wanted to do was pull her into my arms. I let out a deep sigh. I wondered if she'd be at the game tonight. Selfishly, I needed her there. I was going to have a difficult time keeping my head in this game; having her on the sideline would lessen my anxiety. I'd no right to expect that she'd come after everything I put her through. Still, everyone came to our games, and maybe she'd come to watch Tyler play. I could hope.

Shortly the guys arrived and the noise in the locker room

kept me from thinking too much. Everyone was excited about tonight's game. Not only was it our season opener, but we were playing our biggest rival. Also it would mark the team's fiftieth straight win.

"Let's huddle up," Coach shouted, entering the locker room. We all fell silent as we gathered around him.

"Listen up. You've all worked hard for this moment. There's no reason why we can't win this game tonight. I've seen some remarkable plays out there on the practice field. Also, in all my years as a coach I've never seen a team that has as much passion as you. Your teamwork is what sets you apart from all the other teams. Win or lose, I'm proud of your accomplishments. And you should be too." He glanced at us in turn. "As for you seniors, this is your last chance to beat the Spartans on your own turf." He paused. "Now, are you ready to go kick some ass?"

The roar in the locker room was almost deafening. Everyone shouted and banged on the lockers all at once.

"What are you waiting for?" Coach yelled over the noise.

The team shouted again. Everyone grabbed last minute equipment and rushed out to the field. During the commotion, Coach patted me on the back and whispered, "The scouts from Texas Tech are here tonight, son. Do your best." He smiled encouragingly.

"Thank you, Coach." I just hoped I could pull this off.

The stands were full. She had to be here, I thought. I scanned the crowd, trying to find her. It would be impossible to pinpoint anyone. Then a smile broke across my face when I spotted her sitting in the bleachers near the fifty-yard line. She was easy to find after all. She was wearing purple in a sea of green and white, our school colors. She looked right at me. Instantly I knew how stupid I'd been. I couldn't just give her up. I wasn't protecting her at all by lying to her. As soon as this game was over, I was going to find her and tell her the truth. I loved her and nothing else mattered. I just hoped it wasn't too late.

The first half of the game passed quickly. We were in the lead, 14 to 7. I was playing well. Tyler and I had practiced hard this summer and it showed. So far we'd mostly run the ball, but for the second half Coach wanted us to throw. He wanted me to have the opportunity to impress the scouts.

Things started to really heat up in the second half. Before I went back out on the field I looked up and saw Mikayla still sitting there. I knew I could do this. I sprinted out on the field and took my position. We were receiving the ball. It was snapped back and I ran like hell twenty yards down the field and then cut sharply to the left and hooked back around. I looked for the ball and it landed in my outstretched hands. I crossed into the end zone and scored. The stand exploded with cheers. The score was now 21 to 7. Our defense was just as strong as our offense and we stopped the Spartans in three short plays. The rest of the game pretty much followed the same pattern. The final score of the game was 42 to 7. The fans were ecstatic, rushing the field.

My only thought was to find Mikayla. I had to talk to her. I tried to slip away, but Coach approached me with a man wearing a Texas Tech jacket and matching hat. "Dooner," he called. I turned around. "I want to introduce you to the scouts. They want to talk to you."

"Hi, I'm James Muldoon. Everybody calls me Dooner," I said, shaking their hands. *Well, almost everybody.*

"Great game. My name is Cole Johnson. Is there somewhere we can go to talk? It would be nice to sit down and discuss things with you and your parents."

"I'm already eighteen and my parents aren't a part of this decision. We can talk now." I'd already made up my mind. I wanted to do this. The sooner it was done, the sooner I could find Mikayla and try to convince her to give me a second chance. Over the scout's shoulder, I saw her and Pops congratulating Tyler.

"You can use my office," offered Coach.

"Perfect," answered Cole Johnson.

The meeting didn't last long since I knew what I wanted. I happily agreed to their terms. My dream was coming true. I'd be playing for Texas Tech in the fall, far from home. Soon I was walking out to the parking lot alone. The rest of the team had already changed and gone off to celebrate on some dirt road. I wasn't joining them. I had other, more important, plans. I was going to find Mikayla.

When I looked up, I was surprised to see Mikayla leaning up against Old Faithful, looking amazing in a short jean skirt and the purple hoodie I'd seen from the field. My heart skipped a beat. I couldn't believe she was waiting for me. Maybe things would turn out okay after all. I was ready to tell her that I made a huge mistake. I smiled shyly.

Suddenly the still night was filled with the sound of squealing tires. I quickly turned my head. A truck was headed right toward Mikayla, moving way too fast. I yelled for her to move, but instead she froze like a deer in headlights. I knew I wouldn't be able to reach her in time. I dropped my bag and sprinted, running faster than I ever had in my life. I had to protect her. Her scream pierced my heart.

There was a terrible clash of metal against metal. The truck that had been heading right at Mikayla was now wrapped around a light pole not two feet away from where she was still firmly planted. She didn't have a scratch on her. I almost collapsed with relief.

Reaching her, I said, "Oh my God, Mikayla, are you okay?" I wrapped her tightly in my arms before I quickly checked her over to make sure she was really okay. She was trembling with shock, but other than that she seemed fine.

Her eyes locked on the driver. "I think so. Is that....is that...your dad?"

For the first time, I paid closer attention to the truck. "Yes, it is," I exclaimed. What had he almost done?

Carefully, I moved her out of harm's way. "Stay here. I'll be right back. Call the police."

I approached my dad's truck. He was bent over the steering wheel, blood running down his face. He smelled awful. He was banged up, but unfortunately he'd live. His eyes opened.

He immediately zeroed in on Mikayla, who was standing off to the side at a safe distance. Pointing at her, he said, "I told that stupid bitch yesterday when she came by to return your shirt to stay the hell away. I warned her what would happen if I saw her again. She didn't think I was serious. When I came out of the game, she was waiting for you by your truck. I knew it was up to me to make her understand. You'd never have the guts to let her go, you're nothing but a pussy. You'd rather throw away your chance at playing ball. I wasn't about to let that happen." His face was full of pure hatred.

"You're an idiot, Dad. She has nothing to do with whether or not I play college football. I already signed the papers. I'm playing for Texas Tech next fall. Who says I can't have my dream and a girlfriend too? I love her, Dad. And she loves me. Something you'll never understand." Looking at him with disgust, I continued, "You're going to be locked up for a long, long time." Sirens sounded in the distance. They'd be here any minute. "You'll never be able to hurt me or anyone I love ever again."

The cops arrived and loaded my dad into the back of the squad car in handcuffs. We'd have to go down to the station in a few minutes to give our statements, but before we did that there was something more important I had to do.

Walking over to Mikayla, I took her in my arms. "How come you came tonight?"

"Isn't it obvious?"

I shook my head no.

"I couldn't stay away. I knew how much this game meant to you. I wanted to see you play. Even though I'd never been to a football game until tonight, it was easy to see how talented you really are. Pops was sitting next to me, and I began to worry that he was going to have a coronary the way he kept getting so excited every time Tyler would throw you the ball and you'd catch it, even when it seemed near impossible," she gushed, blushing. My heart practically exploded at her words. Usually I got embarrassed when people complimented me, but this felt right. "I had to congratulate you," she added in a quiet voice.

"I couldn't have done it without you. As soon as I saw you sitting in the stands, I knew everything would be okay. It is going to be okay, isn't it?" My hands were shaky. I couldn't lose her now.

She stared at me with her big brown eyes. "I don't know. Can I ask you something?"

"Anything." I nodded my head for her to continue.

"And I want the truth."

I nodded again.

"Are you in love with Liz?"

"What?" I choked. "Why would you think that?" I hadn't expected that question, and I wasn't sure where it came from.

"Emma said that she saw the two of you making out in the secret hook-up corner while I was home puking my guts out." In all that had happened these last few weeks, I had completely forgotten that Liz had tried to kiss me.

"Yes," I answered honestly, and I felt her stiffen. I rushed to explain before I lost her for good. "I was looking for Coach in the gym, when I ran into her. She was totally wasted and she came on to me. She kissed me, but I didn't kiss her back. I couldn't get away fast enough. I'm sure from where Emma was standing it looked bad, but I swear that's the truth. I love you, not her."

"Then why did you say that you were in love with someone else?" She questioned further. I could tell by the look on her face she wasn't completely satisfied with my answer. I had hurt her and she was trying to figure out why,

"I thought it was the only way you'd let me go."

"You're still not making any sense. Why would you want to break up with me?"

"It's complicated." I took a deep breath to gather my thoughts and then continued. "The day that we made love, my dad saw you leave and he threatened to hurt you if I didn't end things. He thought you'd distract me from winning the scholarship and any chance I had at playing pro ball. I thought I was doing what I had to do in order to protect you. I knew my dad would try to follow through on his threats. He thinks nothing of beating my mom. He used to hit us kids too when we were younger. That day he was so angry he punched me, but he quickly realized he couldn't get to me that way any more." She remained silent as I continued. "So he threatened to hurt me the only way he could. He knew hurting you would hurt me. I'm so sorry. When I think about what almost happened here tonight, it makes me sick. I lied to protect you, but all I ended up doing was hurting you. You could've been killed." I paused to catch my breath. "I'm sorry," I sobbed. "Can you ever forgive me?"

"I already have. I love you," she whispered.

"I love you too."

I wrapped my arms around her pulling her close to me. Vowing that I'd never let her go again.

Epilogue

Mikayla

Graduation day had arrived. I stood in my room getting ready to leave for the ceremony. When we first pulled into this town I couldn't wait to get out. I hated the very idea of spending my senior year in Nowhere. I couldn't believe how much had changed in the past 11 months. How much *I'd* changed! Now I didn't want to leave. I'd be going to college in Michigan, a six-hour car ride from here, but Nowhere would always be my home. It's where I'd found happiness and true love.

Giving James my heart was the most amazing thing I'd ever done. We shared so many special moments together this past year. Some of them grand events, like when he stood by my side at the art show in New York City or when I went with him to check out Texas Tech. Other memories were more everyday events, like sitting at the kitchen table working on homework together or cuddling on the on the porch swing. We spent every free moment we had together, talking, kissing, and making love. He was my best friend.

I loved James with my whole heart, but it wasn't all sunshine and rainbows. Mostly because he suffered a lot of guilt for what his dad tried to do to me, blaming himself for not protecting me. I had to keep reminding him it wasn't his fault. The trial was pushed ahead quickly, since everyone thought his dad posed a threat to the community, and after presenting the evidence, a jury found him guilty of attempted murder. It was a difficult time, but we got through it, and it made us even closer.

Going away to college would present new challenges for us. James signed a contract with Texas Tech to play Division I football, while I'd be attending Cranbrook Academy of Art in Michigan. We debated choosing colleges closer to each other, or even closer to home, but in the end we both knew that wasn't the right decision. We believed that if we were true to ourselves, then the rest would fall in place. We planned to try the long distance thing and see what happened. If we were meant to end up together, then we would. Just like when we were fated to meet on that dusty dirt road so many months ago. It would be painful to be far way from each other, we were used to seeing each other every day, but to borrow one of Pops' clichés – distance made the heart grow fonder (or so we chose to believe).

"Mike, are you coming?" My mom yelled up the stairs.

"I'll be right down," I answered, using the last bobby pin to secure the cap to my head, hoping it didn't fall off before it was time to toss it in the air.

I walked down the steps and saw my mom, Emma, and Pops waiting for me.

"Wow, I can't believe it. You're graduating today," my mom said, tears in her eyes. "It feels like yesterday you were starting kindergarten. I wish your dad were here – he'd be so proud." My mom clasped me to her chest and gave me a tight squeeze. It didn't seem like she was going to let go.

"Mom," I said, exasperated.

Finally she released me, and I rolled my eyes. See, some things changed, but other things didn't. My mom and I got along much better now than we did when we moved here, but sometimes I still got annoyed with her. Like right now. Being touchy feely still wasn't my thing.

"You look smart," said Emma, giving me a compliment. We'd probably always have our fights, we just had one yesterday, but we had learned to be friends. Sharing a room, and living in this small town, had changed us for the better. We both finally recognized how lucky we were to have each other to lean on when it counted.

"That's my girl." He winked. Pops didn't have to say aloud that he was proud of me because it was written on his face. He knew I wouldn't want him gushing over me too. That wasn't our style. Instead he turned to Emma and said, "You better brush up on your trivia. Because once Mike leaves, you'll have to follow in her footsteps and help me with the crosswords. I'm getting old, and I can't remember stuff like I used to." Pops didn't need Emma's help on puzzles any more than he needed mine, he was just letting me know it was okay with him for me to move on. Hopefully Emma would seize the opportunity and spend some time with Pops. He was of my most favorite people in the world and I'd miss him dearly when I was away at college. I looped my arm through his as we walked out of the house.

We arrived at school and I headed off to the cafeteria to meet the rest of the class to line up, while my family went to find seats. Since it was a beautiful day, not a cloud in the sky, the graduation was being held outside on the football field. Chairs were set up on the field for the seniors, and the guests sat in the stands. There was more than enough seating for all family and friends who wanted to watch. I felt a sudden rush of nerves as I thought about all those people watching me accept my diploma that would mark the next end of one chapter in my life and beginning of another.

As soon as I stepped into the cafeteria, James greeted me, picking me up off of my feet, and swinging me around. "Hey, beautiful."

"Hi," I said, exhaling.

Putting me back on the ground, he leaned down and kissed me on the lips. I placed my arms around his neck and pulled him closer. Heat spread through me like it always did when James was near. I nipped at his mouth with my teeth, and then parted my lips to welcome his tongue.

Suddenly someone coughed. "There'll be none of that right now. You're still in school." Coach said, coming up behind us. "Just because you'll be graduating in a few minutes, doesn't mean you don't have to follow the rules." I blushed. It was easy to become so wrapped up in James' touch and how good it felt that I often forgot where we were.

"I know you guys were voted class couple and all, but the rest of us don't need you to shove it in our faces," joked Tyler, joining us. He was still searching for that special someone. He broke up with Liz when he found out that she had tried to get it on with Dooner that night in the gym. He had spent the rest of the year playing the field. He still had some growing up to do, especially when it came to girls, but Tyler, Dooner, and I had long settled our differences and had reached a friendly understanding. Tyler had come to respect me for standing up for what I believed in, even when that meant we often disagreed.

I made a few other friends this year too, like Gina Jo from art class, and Sophia who reminded me a lot of Paige. I waved to them as we lined up. The only person who hadn't changed at all was Casey. He was still the most perverted human being I'd ever met. At least Emma had smartened up, dumping Casey after homecoming, when she found him dry humping another girl in the secret make-out corner.

"Okay, everyone it's time to line up," yelled Mr. John, who had volunteered to put us in alphabetical order for the processional. I lined up behind Olivia Martin, and James got in line behind me. Having last names that both began with 'M' worked to our advantage. James pulled me to him and inhaled deeply. He did that a lot lately, as if he was trying to memorize my scent.

A few minutes later we exited the school. I waved to my family as we marched across the field and took our seats. Speeches were given, music was played, scholarships were awarded, and then it was time for the reading of the names of the graduates. After sitting through what felt like an eternity, the assistant principal announced, "Mikayla Mooney." I stood and proudly walked across the stage, receiving my diploma and shaking hands with the principal. I cheered as James was called next. A bittersweet smile formed on my face when he returned to his seat. I was happy to be done with high school, but sad that it meant leaving Nowhere and James. Finally all the names were read and the principal said, "And now I present to you the graduating class of 2012." Right on cue, we all tossed our caps in the air, while everyone on the field and in the stands cheered. I didn't wait for my cap to come back down before jumping into James' arms.

"I love you, James," I said.

"I love you too," he answered. His eyes were the brightest shade of green I'd ever seen them. "We got through this year, and we'll great through the next one too. Whatever the future holds, we'll always be together." He clasped my hands in his, and placed them over his heart.

I knew he was right, and the kiss I gave him proved it. I didn't have a crystal ball, but my heart knew it would belong to James forever.